I0591431

Metaphorosis

August 2022

Beautifully made speculative fiction

Also from Metaphorosis

Metaphorosis

August 2022

edited by
B. Morris Allen

ISSN: 2573-136X (online)
ISBN: 978-1-64076-234-3 (e-book)
ISBN: 978-1-64076-235-0 (paperback)

Metaphorosis
a magazine of speculative fiction

from
Metaphorosis Publishing

Neskowin

August 2022

Queen of Crows

Rachel Ayers

A Queen of Crows

Mag loved the witches' kitchen, though it did not love her back.

There were shelves of cookbooks and spellbooks as well as histories and tales, herbs hung from the rafters, spices in their jars on the shelf. The stone hearth with its tremendous mantel was her favorite place to sit and flip through the pages or sort through the apples or peel the potatoes. The kitchen garden, walled and hidden, was a tidy riot of scents and flavors, and Mag knew them all.

The witches left her alone, often enough, though not idle. Then the sparrows and robins would come and tell her stories of far off places, good witches and dancing princesses, glass slippers, wolves in red capes, and maidens trapped in towers rescued by woodcutters.

She had no sense of her own age, though the witches often called her 'pretty young one,' and she did not know how old she was when she realized that, however unlikely it was, a prince or a woodcutter coming to her rescue would be a great adventure. She was far too timid to imagine undertaking a quest alone, but a brave companion or a true love made her daydreams safer.

Mostly she was too busy to think of such things. The three witches kept her cooking, cleaning, grinding herbs for their spells, and whatever other little task they brought her. She mended for them, read to them from ancient grimoires, and brushed their long, sleek hair.

Nobody followed the road to the witches' cottage. No princes, no woodcutters, nor even big bad wolves, by coincidence or design, wandered by and invited her to be whisked away from the witches and their work.

Mag's entire life might have consisted of nothing more than fairy stories and her little bit of kitchen herbology, except that one summer morning a murder of crows flew in through the window and settled around her, on the counters and the sink and the unlit stove. One particularly fine specimen sat on the rim of the basin where she was doing the washing.

"Shoo," she said.

The crow looked at her, unthreatened.

"If the witches find you in here, you'll be baked into a pie."

The crow cawed. It sounded like laughter.

She answered the crow with a caw of her own. The bird went silent, cocked her head at Mag, formed her opinion of the young woman.

The bird shook her feathers and sent the others back out the window. One, two, three, four. Five crows for riches, Mag had heard the rhyme, so this last one must be their queen.

She got a handful of oats from the barrel and held it out. The crow gave her that doubtful, cocked-head expression again. "Go on, then, your highness," said Mag, and the crow dipped her beak into the heap of seed, tossing her head back to swallow.

"Hardly appetizing, child," the crow told her with great dignity.

"Hmm." Mag thought for a moment, then offered her a dried plum. The Queen Crow took this as well, and seemed to prefer it. She preened for a moment, ignoring Mag, who shrugged and went back to her scrubbing. "Don't want to talk, then? You aren't much company," Mag scolded, but the queen did not deign to answer. When she splashed the crow with a bit of sudsy water, she squawked in indignation, ruffled her feathers, and flew out the window.

Mag laughed and thought no more about it.

A Dance for Two

The Queen of Crows flew back the same evening, as the sun turned the sky the color of ripe plums. Mag was hauling water from the well to the garden. Summer had been hot and hard. Persistent watering had kept the garden flourishing.

The crow flapped noisily from beyond the roof and landed in the cherry tree, greeting Mag with her rough voice.

"Welcome back," Mag said. The crow's eyes followed her to the herb patch beside the kitchen door. She dumped the water out, and when her bucket was empty, the crow flew to the windowsill and appealed to Mag with shining black eyes.

"I haven't any more treats for you," Mag said. "You'll have to earn your supper, just as I do."

"How shall I do that?" the crow asked.

The queen could not haul water, or peel potatoes, or pull the boiling cauldron from the fire. "Sing for your supper, like they say."

The queen cawed, crowed, laughed at that idea. Her throaty, cackling voice was by no means pleasant. Yet Mag found she was pleased by the effort, and went about preparing dinner for the witches, and herself, and the crow.

The queen flew away when the witches returned, tittering and boasting more than any crow ever had. They had their supper in a swirl of merriment which did not reach out to Mag.

When they had gone back to their business, she went into the moonlit garden. A rustle from the cherry tree alerted her: there was the crow, a shadow in the darkness, studying her.

"I've sung for you," the queen cawed. "Will you dance for me?"

"You sang for your supper," Mag countered. "What shall I dance for?"

The queen cocked her head one way and then the other. "For my curiosity," she ventured, which Mag liked, but:

"I don't know how."

"If my singing pleased you, I assure you your dancing will please me."

So she swayed, and turned, and raised her arms to the moon. Witches' chants played in her head, and she moved to their rhythm, shuffling and then spinning with growing grace.

The crow's head bobbed to her movements. She flew to join Mag, becoming impossibly large; touched her wingtips to Mag's outspread hands. Black feathers fell away to reveal black skin, and they danced.

All night they twirled and spun in the garden, laughing and cawing at each other in equal measure.

As the sun peeked over the horizon, the crow caught up the feather cloak she'd cast aside for the dance, changed again in a burst of wings and feathers, and flew away.

Three Witches

The witches called themselves Rozhanitsy, Parca, and Norn. Their business was concocting spells of youth, beauty, and fortune. The vast majority of the works Mag read to them over dinner were treatises or spells on the subject of immortality; her own interests ranged more widely but she had less time for them. The witches were generally merry, more prone to laughter than grumbling. They teased each other mercilessly, and were carelessly cruel to Mag when it amused them.

"What's got you moping, Mag dear?" asked Rozhanitsy, who chattered more than magpies.

Mag had not realized she was acting differently, but she missed the crow queen, who had not returned.

"My friend has gone away," she told them.

Rozhanitsy, Parca, and Norn clucked with glee. "What friend? What friend have you got? Where has your friend gone, pretty young Mag?"

"She is a queen," she told them, holding dignity close as a cloak. "She came and sat in the garden. I gave her some food, and we danced in the moonlight. She left, though, and hasn't returned."

At this, they grew quiet, thoughtful. They consulted amongst themselves, muttering low so that Mag only caught a few words. "If she should return... royalty... by what path could anyone... lest we lose her...."

They turned back to her, three sets of eyes glaring suspicion. Rozhanitsy asked, voice sugary, "Mag, sweet Mag, how did this lady—err, queen—arrive? By the path? Through the woods?"

"She flew in the window with four of her court. Then they flew away again, but she came back alone later."

Norn, eldest of the three and sharpest, narrowed her eyes. "What did this queen of yours look like, Mag?"

"Black as my hair, with bright eyes and a sharp nose."

More murmuring and glances exchanged.

"And how tall was your queen, young Mag?" asked Rozhanitsy.

Mag spanned her hands in front of her.

Their concern turned into a fit of sniggering.

"And how wide her wing-span, your flying queen?" Parca peeked at the others for approval.

Mag held her arms out again.

"And how rough her voice?" asked Rozhanitsy.

Mag cawed an imitation of the Queen Crow.

The witches collapsed in laughter, howling and slapping one another. Mag watched them, her face hot from their teasing.

Parca and Norn, still shaking in amusement, went through the kitchen door and down the hall. Rozhanitsy stayed a moment, and said, "Mag, I hope your friend does return. But crows are tricky, and if she does come back, you should catch her and let us bake her into a pie."

Four Small Losses

Rarely was Mag tempted into an act of disobedience, but in her longing for the Queen Crow to return, she found herself in a sour and disagreeable mood. She burned the cooking and dragged her feet around the garden. forgot the herbal lore she knew in her sleep and mixed up cumin and fennel for the first time in her memory. She did the washing and mending, but so slowly and so ill that she had to do it all twice. She answered the witches' questions in surly tones or grunts.

It went on for weeks, until Rozhanitsy came into the kitchen and asked her what was wrong. Mag shrugged and continued to scrub the stew pot without vigor.

"Dear, pretty Mag." Rozhanitsy drew her away from the sink to sit at the table. "You know that we three care for you, and feed you, and provide for all your needs. All we ask in return is your unquestioning obedience. You understand that, right?"

Mag nodded.

"Well, child, I'd like to believe you, but from the way you've behaved lately, I'm not sure that settles things. What is for dinner?"

Mag had a bit of dough rising for bread; she hadn't thought beyond that. She'd spent the morning reading a tale of a hedgehog who was secretly a prince and tricked the nearby king out of his daughter.

"I see." Rozhanitsy patted Mag's hands, there before her on the table, and then in a quick motion, cut off the little finger of Mag's right hand. The knife had appeared and disappeared so suddenly it might have been magic. Mag stared, numb, at her blood and her pinkie, lying separate from the rest of her.

Rozhanitsy scooped up the finger and studied it for a moment, then tidied it away into her pocket. "Mag, I want you to remember this. It's a moment to help you focus. We're doing very important work and we can't be bothered with cooking and cleaning. We depend on you."

Rozhanitsy bustled out of the kitchen.

Then the pain started, and Mag wailed.

Though the witches had punished Mag before, they had never done anything so permanent. Mag, shocked at this betrayal, gave up thoughts of black birds and night dances. She grew accustomed to the loss, regaining her dexterity once the pain faded. Norn put her finger bones on the mantle, and it was enough to remind Mag of her place. She did not even need to consult the books, once she recalled herself to focus, to concoct a balm to stop the ghost of her finger from itching.

She did have company, an occasional robin or blue jay, but never a crow. She worked up the nerve, finally, and asked for news of the Queen Crow. A sparrow told her that she'd given up her crown and was dancing with ladies-in-waiting in a distant palace. Late one night, an owl told her that the Queen Crow had married a prince, the youngest son of a faraway king.

"Yes, yes indeed." The owl blinked down at Mag's astonishment. "The court of crows flew for seven days, to a kingdom of spiraling towers and bright flowers. A sunny place, with too much daylight. Warm, though."

"I don't understand," Mag protested.

"Oh! Well, the farther south one travels, the warmer the seasons."

Mag crossed her arms. "I meant about the court of crows, and the wedding."

"Ah!" The owl shuffled in her feathers, settling into the crook of the branch.

"There was a ball at the grand palace, a three day extravaganza, where beautiful ladies and handsome men were dancing together, wearing shimmering garments and feather masks. The Crow Queen flew down to join them, and took the form of a woman, and wore her feathers as a magnificent cape. At the end of three nights, the prince was to choose a bride from the revelers."

"I think I know the story," said Mag. Or at least she had heard one like it.

"I did not attend to the details," the owl admitted. "The Crow Queen, however, danced with one lord more than all the others. He wore raiment of gold, radiant as sunlight. His mask was made of the feathers the crows and the ravens, all the darkest birds, and on the third night as the prince claimed his bride, the dark lord slipped off his mask and asked the Crow Queen to be his wife. For he too was a prince of that land, and needed a bride of his own.

"That was many seasons ago, of course. The rest of the court of crows scattered, and it was some time more recent that I heard these tidings."

Mag felt foolish. She had longed for the Crow Queen, who, it seemed, had not given Mag a second thought. She left the owl to watch for mice and voles in the garden and went back to her kitchen hearth.

Mag wept all night, surrounded by the scent of the thyme and rue she'd bundled to dry above the hearth. At dawn, she crept back to her bed in the corner of the kitchen and recited herbal lore to herself until she fell asleep.

Norn was not pleased. She woke Mag, shaking her until the girl sat up and stared at her, blinking in the light.

"Mag," she said, "There was nothing for breakfast, and lunch looks to be missing, too. The kitchen is a mess, and the clothes in the mending heap haven't been touched all day. What do you have to say for yourself?"

"I was sleeping." Mag lay back down and shut her eyes; she was not sleeping, in truth, but dreaming of a life where she was a princess in a tower instead of a servant in a kitchen.

She heard Norn sigh. "Has it been a hard night, child? Have you trouble waking?" Norn took her uninjured hand and gave it a gentle pat. "Let me aid you."

Mag cracked her eyes open in time to see the witch lift the hand to her mouth and bite off the smallest finger.

It hurt immediately this time.

Norn pulled the finger out of her mouth and wagged it at Mag. "You look more bright-eyed already. Now see to your chores."

Mag found her focus once more, and soon after, the new bones were added to the mantle. She grew ever quieter, afraid to lose any more of herself, and continued to do the witches' bidding. When she gathered herbs in the cold light of the full moon she would, sometimes, think of flying away over the garden wall, but no matter her dreams, she did not grow wings; in all the witches' books, the only spells that granted such transformations came at too permanent a cost.

It was a spring evening, more than a year later, when she saw a single sooty black crow winging across the sky. It was too far away to see if it had been the queen, but Mag waved and called to it. The crow fluttered and dipped, landing on the branch where his queen had alighted the night she danced with Mag.

"Stay a while, rest," she said, holding out a handful of dried plums. "Tell me of your queen."

"Oh, our queen, hmph, she is gone quite mad, or so they say." The crow plucked the fattest plum from Mag's palm.

"Mad?" Mag prompted; the bird took his time over the fruit.

"Well, in the way of a creature who cannot be herself," he clarified, chortling over another choice plum.

Mag sighed in sympathy.

"She cannot be cured of her humanity." The crow eyed her suspiciously and then gulped the last plum. "Her husband stole away her feather cloak when she bore him a son, and when she demanded her feathers back, he told her that he couldn't have a wife who would fly away on a whim. She has been searching for her cloak ever since, and has all of us, her *true* court, seeking for another way to change back into her true self. She has tried tinctures and ointments, and consults with wise-women and witches alike. The human courtiers think her quite touched."

The bird cocked his head again, but seeing no more plums forthcoming, bunched his feathers to fly again.

"Wait!" Mag cried, but he was already off, over the garden wall and out of sight. Free as she never could be, the bird awakened a bitter longing in her heart.

She wanted to follow the crow, to find its Queen. For the first time, Mag was desperate to leave, determined to go. She wanted to see more than a tiny garden corner of the world. She wanted more than witches and potions and a tidy little kitchen. She wanted to find her friend.

In front of the cottage was a dark flagstone path. It was not so very long, and then there was the road, stretching into the forest in either direction. Mag set out without so much as an apple for the road, but stopped at the garden gate, unable to decide which way to go, and then a thousand protests clamored in her mind: where would she go, how would she eat, how would she earn her way? *Foolish girl*, she scolded herself.

She sank to the frigid stones, lost within sight of the garden wall she knew so well.

When morning came, Rozhanitsy, Parca, and Norn found her still at the end of the path, shivering in the misty sunlight. They brought her back to her hearth and then Rozhanitsy and Parca left her alone with Norn.

Norn sat beside her. "What's gotten into your head?"

"I want to fly away." Mag hid her face in her hands, felt the ghosts of her smallest fingers tickling her cheeks and wished she hadn't spoken.

"Don't we feed you, and keep you safe? The world is a hard place, and you're safe here, so long as you do what you're told. You understand that, don't you?"

Mag nodded, but did not lift her face.

"You are part of our great work, Mag," Norn told her. "One day we will find our answer, and that will be because you have assisted us. That gives your life meaning. You will find no answer so easy as that in the wider world."

"But I want to see it!" Mag burst out, then clapped her hands over her mouth. She looked at Norn, fearful.

"However much you may wish to fly away, you haven't got wings. Remember your feet? There on the ends of your legs? You'll do better to stay solidly planted, and keep to your work."

This time, Mag was ready for the knife. She jumped away as Norn moved toward her.

"Sisters," Norn said. She did not raise her voice, but they appeared as though they had been waiting for her.

Mag fought them, kicking and thrashing, but she had nowhere to go, and soon they had her trapped. Rozhanitsy and Parca held her, and Norn cut the smallest toe from each foot.

Mag screamed.

Norn took no notice. Mag nearly missed the witch's words over the throbbing of blood through her ears and face. "One for grounding, two for obedience. Remember, Mag."

She remembered, but it was not the last time she attempted flight.

Five Years

On the fifth anniversary of her flying away, the Queen of Crows returned as though only days had passed. She sat on the kitchen mantel, next to Mag's tiny bones, and cawed impatiently at Mag when she did not look up from her chair beside the fire.

"Go away, bird." It was evening; she was nearly finished hemming Norn's new skirt and she wanted to go to bed early.

"Why do you hunch over your work, and speak like an old woman?" the crow asked her. "Your face is not lined, your hair is not gray."

Now she glared at the queen with the full force of her anger and despair. "Why should I be young and happy? Is my life so wonderful? Is my life worth anything at all?"

The crow fluttered, but settled again. "Your life is hard, and I owe you an apology, for leaving you and more. Will you listen to my story, and decide if you can forgive me?"

Mag pushed herself out of the chair and hobbled outside. There was now a shackle on each ankle, and the chain between them was short. Her missing toes ached as winter bowed to spring.

She sat on the stoop. The moon was already in the sky, glowing orange on the horizon. The witches were gone to some revelry or mischief. Mag did not know when they would return.

The crow followed her and landed on the garden path, inky against the pale flagstones.

"Do you remember the night we danced in the moonlight?" she asked.

Mag laughed; not happily.

"When I watched you dance, I learned how to take off my feathers and stand as a woman." From her place before Mag, she shook herself. Then a cloak of feathers fell away, and she held it in human hands. She sat cross-legged on the stony path. "I flew far away that night, afraid of what I had, for that moment, become. Humans are tricky, confusing creatures, and I had felt things I did not understand. I flew until the sun rose, then I slept. When I woke, I did not know where I was, only that I was far outside my territory."

She told Mag of her young prince, who had seemed a brilliant novelty but had twisted her life into a cage. Of her search for a restoration, and the hedge-witch who had advised her. All this Mag knew, but now the Queen told her in greater detail, and her heart twisted as she remembered her own longing to go to her friend's aid.

"For a time, I was lost in despair. But news came to me that the queen was, at last, expecting a child. When the babe was born, my husband said to me: 'Destroy the babe, wife, and I'll return your cloak.' This was the first proof I had that he knew where it was, and I became furious. I called him an evil wizard. He said there was but one way for me to get what I wanted, and at last I told him I would do as he bid."

Mag startled at this, horrified.

"I went by night to the queen's chamber, and stole her little daughter. The child was peaceful in my hands, and as I gazed at her, I conceived a great love in my heart. I could no more harm her than I could hurt my own son. I took the girl deep into the forest, to a hedge witch I had met in my quest to return to my true form.

"When I told my husband the deed was done, he clapped and laughed, and I saw the shadow of the beauty that had drawn me to him. 'Now fulfill your end of the bargain, husband.'

"He tore his pillow from our bed. Black feathers fluttered in the air around him. 'What have you done?'

" 'I used the life in them to conceive our child.'

"I knew, then, of one magic to try, though I did not know if it would work."

Mag watched the queen's gentle fingers close into fists. She continued, as though she dare not stop now.

"I went to the queen and revealed all that I knew. She called the king, who was grieved at his brother's treachery, but when his eyes met mine I could see that he was not surprised.

"In the morning my husband was tied to a stake in the courtyard. I carried my son forward, and then drew from a sack all of my beautiful black feathers. I spread them on the ground around him while my child watched.

"I raised my head, and called out in my true voice. My lord's face turned to fear as I summoned my own court. First a single crow appeared, and then two more, and then a whole murder. They dove at the man I had married, pecking and clawing at him. As he bled, each drop fell upon a feather, restoring the vitality he had stolen from me. The king and queen clung to each other, turning their faces away. Our son cried and reached forward to touch my cloak, and in that instant was transformed into a crow.

"When the last breath left my husband's body, my cloak was complete, but for a ragged corner which had formed around my son. At last I could stretch my wings again. I took to the air, and my son followed, and the other crows too, and we did not look back."

Mag touched the cloak. It was sleek and smooth; no trace of the blood-magic remained.

The crow queen gestured, and Mag made out a fluttering in the trees outside the garden fence. There was her court. One of the birds was smaller, his feathers not quite as black; bits of baby down still showed in patches.

"Why did you come back?" Mag asked.

"When I was only a crow, I didn't understand why you were here. Now that I have been trapped, I know what it looks like. I have come to set you free." She stopped, then, almost shyly, "If you wish to come with me."

Mag touched the shackles at her ankles. "How?"

The queen raised her arm, gave a signal, and the crows left the trees. They flowed past in a rush of wings and wind, and flew into the house.

Silence fell while they waited.

The first crow returned with a hair pin from Rozhanitsyi's dresser, a bit of metal gleaming in the moonlight. Mag picked it up and looked at the Queen Crow.

"Wait," she assured Mag.

The second crow flew out and dropped a coin at their feet. Mag had seen Parca twiddling with it, shining it through her fingers, a few evenings earlier.

A third crow came back with Norn's little mirror, the one she used to look at faraway places. Mag caught it before it broke on the flagstones.

The three crows looked at their little collection, then at the queen. They ruffled their feathers in a kind of shrug, and flew back into the house.

The crows of the Queen's court repeated this until Mag had a little pile of glittering objects at her feet.

At last, the Queen's son returned. In his beak he carried a tiny key, duller in color than the other objects. Mag recognized it.

The little bird landed in her lap and held it until she took it from his beak. She fit it to the lock at her ankle, and the Queen Crow reached forward and turned it.

The shackle opened with a crack.

Six Days

"Come away, come away," the crows urged. "Before they return."

Mag took nothing with her. She followed the crows' singing; they cawed to her from the trees ahead. She found she was able to keep a steady pace, in spite of leaving her toes on the witches' mantel.

They walked all through the night and into the next day. Mag felt lighter with every step away from the witches' cottage. Every new sight refreshed her, whether it was a beautiful lady rushing by in a gilded coach, or an old man ambling along with a load of firewood, or a young lad guarding miniscule treasures in his wary fists.

They passed through the woods, and then a little hamlet, and then onto a broader road. The Crow's son joined them for a time, utterly silent, toddling along, then took to the air again. The Queen Crow herself seemed content to walk with Mag, watching her take in every scene along their way with as much delight as she took in watching her son discover new things.

They stopped for the night, and the Queen Crow paid for a room, telling the innkeeper that Mag was her sister. Mag could not imagine where she kept the coins when she changed to a crow. She winked at Mag as she shone the money through her clever fingers.

Though she was exhausted, Mag was too full of the day to sleep. So the queen told her stories, from her life, or that she had heard, long into the night. Mag fell asleep dreaming of distant places, cottages on chicken's legs and magic lamps.

Five days more, they continued in this fashion. The farther Mag got from the witches' cottage, the more certain she became that this was real, but even so, she did not ask where they were going: a destination was too much to believe.

Then she heard laughter.

Seven for a Secret

The witches came sweeping over the land in a dark wind, finding her as easily as if she were still in the kitchen. They stole her away from the Queen Crow while she slept, head tucked under her wing, and brought Mag back to her little kitchen hearth, and all her fighting and thrashing and cursing made them laugh more.

"Mag, Mag, we must have you! We are almost at the end of all our hard work! Don't you want to know what happens?"

"I want to leave," Mag said. She would run farther this time.

They pulled her into the kitchen and sat her at the table. She waited for them to chain her, but they did not. Instead they pointed to the cauldron, where a murky stew was brewing.

"There it is, my dear," said Rozhanitsyi. "The key to our immortality, at last. Everyone dies, but we will break our fate. After all our long preparations, we have only to test it."

"I don't want to be immortal." Mag leaned away from their gazes.

They cackled. "Oh you won't, pretty Mag," said Parca. "We have undergone intense rituals, sacrificed many things, and prepared our bodies. The potion will not make you immortal."

"Then why do you want to test it on me?" she asked. She wondered if she could bolt for the door. One look at their faces killed the thought; they would catch her before she made it outside.

"If you take it, we can observe the effects, and match them with our studies. Then we will know the potion has been properly prepared," Norn explained. "It is very delicate; a single wrong ingredient will unbalance the whole thing. But I promise you, Mag, you will smile if you taste it. And after you test it, we will never ask anything of you again." She looked at the other witches. "What say you, sisters? This last task and Mag may go wherever she wills?"

They smiled and nodded. "Yes, Mag," said Parca, and Rozhanitsy added, "Nothing more will we ask of you!"

"I may go freely if I test your potion?" Surely it was a trick, some mischief, but they gazed at her earnestly.

Rozhanitsy nodded. "We will have no more need of you."

"How long will it take?" Mag asked, suspicious.

They hesitated. Then Norn said firmly, "One day. We must observe the effects for a full day, to be certain."

"And it won't hurt me?"

"It will make you smile," Rozhanitsy said again.

"Very well, I will test it. Then I never want to see you again," Mag said.

"You won't have to," Parca said. She looked a bit hurt.

Norn dipped a spoonful of the stuff and brought it to Mag's mouth, feeding her like a babe.

It did not taste as bad as it looked; bitter, but with the sharpness of fresh herbs. She swallowed, and waited.

It started in her stomach, a cramp, a slight discomfort. She pressed her hands against her belly. Norn, Rozhanitsy, and Parca were nodding, smiling: pleased.

And it spread, a hot cramping pain, worse than anything Mag had ever known. She tumbled out of her chair, collapsing to the floor as fire and chills raced through her body. She gasped at the shock of it and crumpled beside the hearth.

"Very good," Norn said, checking the sheaf of notes she held. "It is going as I expected."

"We will check on you soon," Rozhanitsy said, patting Mag's head. Each touch sent daggers through her skull.

The witches left her alone. They didn't need to chain her; she couldn't even crawl.

The Queen Crow flew in through the window. She transformed in an instant and knelt beside Mag. "What have they done?"

Mag could not answer.

The queen touched her face with feather-light fingers. She studied the cauldron, the spoon resting on the table. "They are killing you."

Mag nodded and squeezed her eyes shut.

"Come away," the crow said. "Hurry," she said.

Mag could not move. "Stay," she pleaded.

An hour later, Rozhanitsy returned. The crow flew away before she entered the room. "Another dose, my dear. This one should go a bit better." She fed Mag another spoonful.

The effect spread through her body again. She grew heavy, as though the earth had decided to draw her closer. The pain chasing through her body thumped its now-familiar rhythm. It was harder still to move.

When Rozhanitsy left, the crow came back.

Mag knew, then, of one last magic to try, though she did not know if it would work. "May I have a feather?" Mag asked.

The queen plucked one, long and dark as night, from her cloak. Mag pointed toward the cauldron, and the crow dropped it into the potion.

"Come back here," Mag whispered, "if you will. It helps, I think." She reached out a leaden hand. The queen returned and held her fingers carefully until they heard Norn coming into the kitchen.

Each time Norn fed her a sip, the potion grew clearer, as though Mag were draining the color from it. Mag sank and then floated, was sick and then hot and then numb. Sometimes Norn asked her how she was feeling; sometimes she was able to answer.

After each dose, the Queen Crow or one of her court added a feather, which disappeared with no more than a sizzle and wisp of light. It was, she reasoned, no more risky than doing nothing; she did not believe the witches would let her leave alive.

"One more taste after this," Norn said, late in the night, and fed Mag a spoonful that made her tingle all over.

The Crow returned, and prepared to drop another feather into the potion; a downy feather from her son. "No," Mag said.

She tipped her beak at Mag quizzically.

She pointed at the mantle. The queen found Mag's finger- and toe-bones where the witches had left them.

"Yes," she managed.

The queen added them to the concoction, which hissed and boiled for a moment before settling again to the clarity of fresh rainwater. "What do we make, Mag?" she asked.

Mag tried to explain the muddled lore in her mind; the thoughts chased around each other and would not leave her mouth. She was not even certain that her idea would work, if the witches' potion was too strong for her to change—but another potion of transformation, another spell to change the form of a life—it was all she could try. The crow watched her and then nodded thoughtfully. "You need not speak, then, my dear," she told Mag. "I will wait and see."

At sunrise, all three witches returned. Norn gave her one last dose. "How does that suit you?"

Mag took an easy breath. The last of the aches and chills faded away, and the various discomforts dissipated. Pleasure— and then euphoria—filled her senses.

"It's… wonderful," she said, and felt a grimacing smile grip her cheeks. The room faded; she could not focus her eyes.

"We'll be back in an hour," Parca said, "to move the body."

The others shushed her, and they left Mag alone again.

She felt glorious: as though light were pouring out of her, as though she were drinking honey-wine gone to her head.

She realized that the Queen Crow was weeping into her human hands, dark hair spilling over her face. "Why are you crying?" Mag asked.

"Because you are dying, and I have just begun to know you."

She looked down at herself in wonder: was this dying? Then she realized that she was truly looking down at herself from above. Her skin was turning gray, her eyes were growing dull. There was a smile on her lips, but the queen was right: she was dying. The witches would let her go because they had no use for the dead.

So then, if that body did not hold her mind any longer, where was Mag? She shook herself, felt the soft rattle of feathers tested for the first time.

The Queen Crow held out a hand to her and she alighted. "Hello there, Maggie," she murmured. "You are still here."

"Did you not know why I asked for your feathers?" Mag asked.

"No." She stroked Mag with her other hand. "I thought you were lost."

Mag preened, testing her feathery body. She was spirit-light; a wisp of a creature, hardly more substantial than a cloud. It was all she had left, but it was a body, and one that could fly. She did not know how long it would last; but then, no one ever did. "Hurry," she said. "Help me."

She flew out to the garden and plucked elderberries, evil's bane; they bled red on their white blossoms as she tugged them free. She winged back and dropped them into the cauldron. They disappeared in the clear potion, with nothing but a wisp of steam to show they'd ever been.

Next, flax and horehound, for purification. The other crows, under their queen's command, followed her lead, around the garden and back again. Now rue and vervain, cleansing herbs, the potion still and clear as water. Rosemary: distinctive, purifying. And last, ague root, also called crow corn, hex breaker, ritual uncrosser. Her beloved kitchen and garden had never loved her back, but she knew every herb and its effect. With every gleaning from the garden and from her years studying their books, she bent the potion to her own purpose.

The witches returned to the kitchen, a dead girl, and a new potion.

Mag lingered under the eaves. "See how she smiles, even in death," Norn said. "See how her skin is like stone. The potion has worked as described on an unprepared mortal. It is ready for us, now."

"I thought she'd grow smaller," said Rozhanitsy.

"I thought she'd be wrinkled," said Parca.

"And I thought our preparations would be done decades ago," Norn said sternly. "Let us finish this thing, sisters."

They drank until the cauldron was emptied.

Mag fluttered to the trees, where the Queen was waiting with her court and her son. They welcomed her into their murder as the witches steamed and shrieked. Mag's spell scoured them of the death they'd twisted back to life, cleaned them of the wrongness they'd collected and clutched over the years. She did not think there would be anything left of them after that.

She did not stay to see.

The Queen Crow's court flew away: one as white as a dove, as there-and-gone as a wisp of cloud. Housewives and hedge witches watched them pass overhead. Some counted six and some counted seven, and all kept their secrets to themselves.

See Rachel Ayers's story "Queen of Crows" online at Metaphorosis.
If you liked it, leave a comment. Authors love that!
Remember to subscribe to our e-mail updates so you'll know when new stories are posted.

About the story

There is a folkloric rhyme about counting crows or magpies, and what each number of birds signifies.

A question for the author

Q: Are you an outline or discovery writer?

A: I have aspirations to be an outline writer. I've written an outline once! Mostly, though, I find I don't know enough about the story to do the outline until after I've written the story. I affectionately call myself a pantser, as in "by the seat of my pants".

About the author

Rachel Ayers lives in Alaska, where she writes and hosts shows for Sweet Cheeks Cabaret, daydreams, and stares at mountains. She has a Master's in Library and Information Science, which comes in handy at odd hours. She is a regular contributor at tor.com and she obsesses over fairy tales more than can possibly be healthy. She shares speculative poetry and flash fiction (and cat pictures) at patreon.com/richlayers.

richlayers.net, @richlayers

The Hissing Trees

Ian Donnell Arbuckle

The biovin Charis heard the rumors about the messenger long before he arrived at her laboratory. The watergirls whispered that he had come from the Calomlands, further east than their maps could show with any accuracy. He bore an important text for the yurchief, said one of the boiler technicians, though nobody had heard even a hint of the contents. One of the guard faithful let slip that the messenger had personally angered the yurchief and had been restrained almost immediately upon his arrival.

All took care to mention that he appeared to be on his last legs, having collapsed just on their borders, and that his hideous body bore the bloat of illness.

The yurchief's orders came to Charis through the precise, bored imperiousness of one of the younger faithful, his voice struggling to hold up the import of the words without cracking beneath the strain. "The biovin Charis is to extract from the messenger the content of the message. There will be no tolerance for fault, no allowance for failure."

Charis accepted the order with a calm nod, reserving her questions for the voice inside her. Why was she, a biovin, being tasked with this? Charis had none of the skills of the cryptonos, and she knew her political acumen was inadequate for the delicate job of interrogation. It had, in fact, been the cause of her effective banishment to this lab in the canyons, deep in Sound territory and far from the yurchief's gatherings.

She hadn't minded the isolation, and instead considered it something of a blessing. A place had been found for her where she could contribute the bread of her skills to the feast of her people. For the last few years, she had been reviewing the pharmaceutical work of her predecessor in the role, improving some compounds and helping to fabricate tabs for the yurchief and those in his pull. Most of the changes were incremental, glacial things that nevertheless gave her a continuing satisfaction that each small, stable adjustment maintained the whole.

Rarely did she see the results of her efforts, but she knew they were successful, if for no other reason than because the yurchief permitted her to continue her work undisturbed and untroubled. For the most part. She liked her work, and her work accepted her in silence. Days could pass between opportunities for her to speak with another living creature. She liked that just fine.

"What am I to do with this foreign messenger?" She only asked it aloud after the young guard faithful had left to deliver her note of obedience back to the yurchief. She kept asking it, mostly to the quiet spaces in her head, until she got her first look at the messenger himself the next day.

Two more of the guard faithful escorted him into her lab. The rumors had been inadequate. He was repulsive to behold, his body a battlefield of open sores, wild lumps of tumors, and ulcerous cavities.

He hunched beneath rags that scraped over uneven shoulders, blood and pus staining the stinking fabric. His face could hardly bear an expression, given how the flesh had mottled and bulged with disease. Growths settling from his brow and rising up from his cheeks trapped his eyes in a deep valley, but within all that they shone a clear blue and his gaze was direct. He seemed to study Charis with at least as much intensity as she did him.

He wore shackles on his wrists which, though loose, had nevertheless left deep red welts where they touched his skin.

"Am I to cure him?" asked Charis, taken aback.

"You are to extract from the messenger the content of his message." It was the same instruction, repeated. Though it came from a different pair of lips, the tone was the same as the first time she had heard it: a committed, tremulous tenor.

"By means of...?" Charis prompted.

"There will be no tolerance for fault—"

"I understand," interrupted Charis, who could not abide time wasted on repetition.

"I may be able to illuminate somewhat," said the messenger. "If I may?" His voice was pitched low and each word carried a polite deference. There was a gentle if unpleasant rumble beneath them. Charis recognized the sound as betraying the presence of some fluid or phlegm in the lungs.

"I would appreciate that," she said.

"Of course." The messenger glanced to either side before continuing. Neither of the faithful made a move to stop him. "You see, I carry the message inside my cells." He raised limp hands to indicate the deformities about his body. The obvious effort of doing so was not solely due to the weight of the shackles, Charis guessed.

"Spun into the helices?" she asked, after running the messenger's words through the sieve of her mind.

The messenger's lips twisted into what may have been a smile or a grimace. "Essentially, yes," he said. "The text of the message is encoded among the information there, intended to be read only be those able to retrieve it. Do you think you can?"

Charis nodded faintly, the motion diminishing like the vibration of a loose cord. "Doing so will not relieve you of the cancer, you understand."

"I defer to your expertise," replied the messenger. His lungs convulsed and a wet coughing fit overcame him.

Charis frowned sharply at the faithful. "You may leave him with me. Tell the yurchief I will begin work immediately." With gratitude they were unable to conceal, the two young men backed away, then turned and left the laboratory. The messenger, unable to convey much with expression, cleared his throat and raised his arms a second time, this time in supplication. The chains on the shackles clanked heavily.

"May these be removed, my friend?"

Charis gave him a long look, calculating, and then shook her head. "I would be uncomfortable doing so at this time, though I do have some gauze I will insert as a buffer."

"I would appreciate that, thank you," said the messenger, echoing her tone from earlier. The mimicry didn't escape Charis' notice, but she was unsure of what to do with the information and set it aside for the time being.

"Please have a seat," she said, indicating the only chair in the room. It had five metal spokes at its base, each ending in a black caster. It rolled slightly as the messenger sank onto it.

"Thank you," he repeated.

Charis turned away to retrieve the roll of gauze from her supplies. The laboratory was a single, large space, lit in part by fluorescent tubes that hung low over a repurposed dining table, the sort one might expect to find in a chieftain's meeting hall. The table bore the wreckage of old electronics and automators, salvaged and scavenged and in various states of repair. A workstation idled at the center of one side, three wide monitors standing as bulwark against the junk. A dozen fans hummed away.

Beyond the sharp radius of the artificial lights, gray filtered sun sifted down from two high windows, one set to the north and the other to the south. Tree branches tapped against panes which had never been cleaned.

The walls were lined with mismatched shelves. The only thing each shared in common was how deeply they bowed under the weight of the materials Charis and her predecessors had collected. As much as was possible, the shelves had been kept tidy. Boxes and containers were arranged with clear separations and angles, as if snapped to an invisible grid.

Charis returned with the gauze. She cut two lengths and taped them around the messenger's wrists. She stood back as he adjusted the fall of the metal bracelets. He nodded once to her.

"Thank you again, my friend," he said.

"My name is Charis." She forestalled the smile that appeared to be growing on his lips with one raised finger. "I'm telling you this so you can call me something other than your friend."

"I understand," said the messenger.

"May I examine you?"

"Of course, Charis. I am an open book. Would you like me to move over toward the light?"

"Yes, if you would."

The messenger rolled the chair over toward the pool of fluorescent light with a series of kicks. He almost looked as if he were having fun. The joints of the chair squeaked with each movement.

Charis sat on a bench next to him and held him steady, spinning the chair slowly like a potter with a fresh lump of clay. "Which is the original tumor?" she asked, letting her eyes travel up and down his body.

"Ah, an interesting question. You're worried the message may not have been copied faithfully during metastasis, yes?"

Charis' first answer was a distracted half-nod. The messenger's back was to her now and she noted the dampness of blood across his shoulders. "Yes," she said, upon realizing she had turned him so that he could no longer see her.

"The message was originally encoded in my liver cells," the messenger said. "The tumors came after, I'm afraid."

"Hmm. I think I might biopsy some of these ones that are more easily accessible first."

"Whatever you think best, Charis, my friend."

It took some hours for Charis to prepare her equipment and to sterilize her tools using the little coal-stoked autoclave. During all that time, the messenger sat patiently. Only the occasional rattle of his chains as he adjusted his position called attention to him. Other than that, he remained silent except to answer Charis' minimal questions.

As Charis staged her surgical tray, though, he spoke up. "Did you build that yourself?" He nodded at the autoclave.

"I designed it," said Charis. "I'm untrained in smithing, though. The yurchief had it built to my specifications."

"He must trust you very much."

Charis searched the messenger's eyes for any sign of sarcasm. "No, that wouldn't be accurate to say," she corrected him with a shake of her head. "I already consume twice my energy allotment just running the refrigeration for the compounds and samples. He was unwilling to grant me more for the superheating. 'Fire or ice, biovin,' he said. One or the other. But he did eventually appreciate my ingenuity more than he did my complaints, I believe."

The messenger nodded. "A true leader."

Charis smiled in spite of herself, then clamped down on it as quick as a breath. She sat again on the bench beside the messenger and positioned her tray close to hand. "I could begin with one of the tumors on your neck, but I think I would prefer to examine your lymphs, if you'll permit it."

"Of course."

"I'll have to remove your shirt."

"If you'll do me the favor of being gentle, I have no objection."

It was hardly a shirt, more of a rough sack with holes for head and arms. "I'll have to cut it away," she said.

"Good. Let's be rid of the foul thing," said the messenger. "Burn it, for all I care."

Charis reached for her shears and turned the messenger in his chair so she could begin to work on the fabric across his shoulders. It took some effort to lift the garment away from his skin, stuck as it was with the gum of drying blood. The messenger inhaled sharply through his teeth.

"I apologize," said Charis. "I have some sugar cane, but I hoped to save that for the surgical sites."

"It's all right," said the messenger through gritted teeth. "Just talk to me. What is sugar cane?"

Charis paused for a moment, then continued at her task, cutting straight down from the middle of the neckline, following the path of the spine. "It's a compound my predecessor taught me. It deadens pain where injected."

"An anesthetic," said the messenger, nodding. "It's all right. We can save that for when it's really needed."

"May I ask—" Charis began, but silenced herself with a shake of her head.

"You may. I insist," said the messenger after a pause.

"What sort of message is worth the toll on your body?" Charis finished her cut and spread the shirt apart, lifting it with care from the messenger's shoulders. She nearly gasped at what she saw.

His back bore a few growths, rising close to his backbone, but worse than them were the dozens of whip strikes layered over his skin. Few of them had healed fully; none had healed well. Some were still oozing. The worst of them lay across his shoulder blades.

"I don't believe it was intended to take a toll at all," said the messenger. He shifted his toes on the floor, turning himself slowly until he could look at Charis in the eyes. "The 'biovins' back home did warn that there were risks, but perhaps this cancer has been fated in me since long before I was given the message, or came upon me after. It would have been nice to arrive here sooner, of course. I'm afraid I was delayed."

"Delayed by—"

Charis' words were cut off by the sound of her laboratory doors slamming open. The yurchief stamped into the room. He stood taller than six feet, broad in his shoulders but narrow in his face. Sealskins draped around his shoulders. Though he was proud of the skins, and of his own prowess in the hunting and killing of the beasts, Charis had often thought that they made him look as if he were forever carting around a pile of filthy laundry. His long hair had been stained red with choke cherries, several days ago by the smell of it.

He crossed the floor to Charis and the messenger before his two guard faithful attendants had even taken station beside the door. "Well?" he demanded, breathing in and holding it. "What is the message?"

"I have only just begun, yurchief," said Charis, lowering her gaze to the floor. "It will take time to extract the samples and then to put them in sequence. I have not practiced this, nor exercised the tech since my predecessor first instructed me in its use. And then I do not know how long it will take to decode the message into plain words, if we are able to retrieve it fully." She met the messenger's own downcast eyes and they held the moment shared between them. Charis got the impression that the messenger had told all of this to the yurchief already.

"I'm deaf to your excuses, biovin," said the yurchief. He curled one finger, rank with the smell of hide and sweat, beneath her chin and lifted her face. "Where is my message?"

"It's coming, your 'ness," she said.

"Good. You have one week. I depart this afternoon to visit the borders. Upon my return, I expect to hear my message."

"But that's—"

The yurchief's hand shifted and his fingernails suddenly bit into the soft flesh of her neck. "One week. If you are worried about fatigue, I grant you the boon of my speed. But not too much, understand?"

"Yes, yurchief."

"Good." He slackened his grip but left the tips of her fingers brushing the skin where bruises would soon form. Then he whirled, washing them in the stink of rancid oils. He snapped at his guard faithful, and the three of them swept out into the night. The laboratory door hung open behind them. A roar of laughter drifted in along with a cool breeze.

Charis went to the door, softness in her every step and motion, and closed it quietly.

"He is a storm among men," said the messenger.

She gave only half of a nod and then returned to his side. "He is not of this place," she said. "He came to us when I was young, and none among us can match him in prowess."

"I've known a few like him," said the messenger. "They do not allow for patience in the movement of things. They thrive in the center of the current, not in the eddies and back-drafts of life. Usually, I wish them well, since they will be long gone before I come to rest." He cleared his throat, which seemed to take more effort than he expected. He ended up spitting a wad of phlegm into the rags that had been his shirt. "He is one of many."

Charis withheld her hands from his skin until his shaking had subsided. Then she began to probe the sores on his back.

"What is the boon of his speed, may I ask?" said the messenger.

"It's a compound my predecessor held the recipe for. I've made some improvements. It keeps the mind alert and blots out weariness from the body."

"Ah. The good stuff," said the messenger. He gasped as Charis' thumb brushed one of the long welts.

"I apologize," she said.

"Please, don't pay me any mind. We have a job to do."

Charis nodded and continued. The signs of infection had spread beneath and around many of the welts, but the discharge was white-becoming-yellow. Treatable. "You said you were delayed reaching us. What happened?"

"It's a long story."

"Oh. You don't have to—"

"May I have some water before I begin?"

"Of course." On the way back from fetching a mug and filling it, Charis retrieved some more strips of clean gauze and a clay pot of salve. The messenger accepted the water gratefully and drank it down in one long gulp, suppressing a rising cough midway through without removing his lips from the mug.

"You shouldn't waste your time," he said, wiping his lips with the back of his hand and nodding at the salve and bandages.

"It may ease your discomfort," said Charis.

The messenger shrugged his agreement. "You're the doctor. Excuse me, the 'biovin'."

Charis moved around him and began carefully applying the salve to the worst infections.

The messenger took a deep breath and began his story. "Between here and the Calomlands, there are three great changes in the land. First, coming from my home, there is a wide plain where sharp ravines scar the flat grasses like claw marks left by enormous beasts. On the other side of those plains, there is a mountain range, peaks taller than any you have around here, but colored gray and white only. Stone and ice. Beyond them is the dwindling forest, plenty green but sparse and thinning. Then comes the mist and the deepness of the bay here—my apologies, the 'Sound'.

"I left my home at the end of winter, hoping to reach and cross the mountain range before the next winter's snow could fall. And I very nearly did.

"My path through the mountains brought me past another tribe. They were not the intended recipients of my message, and I thought it better not to announce my presence to them, so I skirted their holdings and attempted an uncharted route down to the foothills. I was... unsuccessful.

"This tribe—they referred to themselves as the Mallers—caught up with me before I could get far. They set upon me at night, while I was groggy with the cold, and bound me hand and foot. They took me to the edge of a deep canyon between two plateaus and tossed me into a hole a ways back from the precipice, three times as deep as I am tall. There were a dozen others in that hole, all of them ragged and filthy and scared. Our dialects weren't in complete agreement, but before the night was out we were communicating and I learned that I had been pressed into the service of a mighty feat of engineering. The Mallers were building a bridge between the two plateaus. It was a massive thing, indeed."

There was a brief silence while the messenger cleared his throat and gathered his thoughts. While he did, Charis refilled his mug of water. He accepted it and sipped it less greedily than before.

"How long did they keep you there?" Charis asked.

"Three winters," said the messenger, nodding as he heard Charis' involuntary gasp. "And this illness did not rest idle during that time. By the end of it, everyone looked upon me with revulsion."

"They gave you no rest, despite your condition?"

"During my time there, I saw others forced to work until their hearts stopped. My condition, as it worsened, did nothing but earn me a few lashes for my deficiencies."

"'A few'," Charis scoffed.

"Is it so different here?" asked the messenger. "I noted gibbets along the roads. And my guards may have muttered a threat or two that seemed downright believable, not to mention the indignities the yurchief impresses on his prisoners."

There was silence while Charis' face fell. "No," she admitted. "It's not so different here." She took a breath and made a decision before letting the air escape. She crossed to her work table and trailed her fingers over the tools there until she found what she was looking for. Returning to the messenger, she sat and spun him to face her, pulling his shackles forward so she could bend over them with a pick and tension wrench at the ready.

"How did you escape?" she asked while she worked.

"Through no effort of my own." The messenger chuckled. "One night, as we were returning to our pits, an electrical storm lit up the horizon. I've never seen anything like it. It takes much longer to describe than it did to witness. The flashes of lightning clawed through the sunset, but the air healed behind them in an instant. The thunder cracked from one end of the mountains to the other, but the echoes lived on—it seemed like forever. The colors and the intensity were so new, I felt curiously blessed.

"My pit-fellows and captors were likewise stunned. I don't believe anything like that has been seen before. But we only watched for a few moments before the Mallers returned to the task at hand and dumped us for the night. The storm continued, though we couldn't see it."

"Was the pit covered?" asked Charis.

"Most nights, no, but in times of inclement weather the Mallers were kind enough to lay sheets of scrap metal over us to keep out the worst of the rains or snows."

Charis glanced up into a sardonic curl of the messenger's lip and answered it with a nod of understanding. The lock clicked on one of the shackles and she moved to the other.

"So, we were covered that night, listening to the howl of wind and catching odd geometries of brilliant light through the cracks as the storm drew closer. At the height of its fury, it sounded as if we were directly under a waterfall, as if a million gallons of whitewater were bludgeoning the stone around us. We could feel it down to our bones.

"There were screams, but maybe only in my imagination. I don't know how I could have heard them over the racket. To be so small and so vulnerable dead center in the gaze of an unstoppable enemy... I was terrified. The air shook with so much chaos it became difficult to breathe. I buried my head in my hands. But then the clamor only seemed to grow louder. I looked up—I think, despairing, I was determined to stare into the eye of the storm and force it to blink, or some fool thing. Instead what I saw was that the cover of our pit was... disintegrating.

"The jailers had pinned it into the stone with metal hooks, so it hadn't blown away in the winds, but now there were holes appearing all over it. Not just holes, but slashes, rips, patches going threadbare as if the steel were no more than silk. Right before my eyes, it vanished. There was only darkness above, but I could hear a long hush, like swift water, uninterrupted, but somehow more brittle.

"While I sat there, dumbfounded, trying to understand what I was seeing, I heard a scream rise above the lessening wind and that susurrus. A moment later, a body tumbled into the pit. It was one of our captors. I, alone, edged closer to inspect the remains. I couldn't say where he had been trying to run to, or why, but he did not make it. His armor was gone, and the clothes beneath it too, blasted away. His skin and muscles had been flayed, laying open his back to the bones."

Charis felt the lock release on the other manacle and lifted the shackles away from the messenger. He rested his hands on his knees and flexed his fingers.

"What could do such a thing?" Charis asked. "I've heard reports of swarms of insects, but none have mentioned the devouring of flesh. Vegetation, only. A human enemy, perhaps, using the storm as concealment?"

The messenger shook his head. His eyes glittered; clearly, some part of him enjoyed having the information that Charis was after. "I appreciate your theories, Charis, but I'll tell you the truth of it from my observations. You see, that unusual, godlike lightning must have been strong enough and hot enough to melt the gravels and stones into glass, while the winds tumbled that glass until it was atomized, razor sharp particles flying at well more than speeds I can measure. A storm of glass, scouring the mountainsides clean…"

Charis could see it in her mind, a glittering, glowing billow of inarguable power. "Amazing," she whispered.

"It truly was. And the next morning, after everything settled, we were able to cooperate to pull ourselves out of the pit. None of the Mallers had survived the night. Their huts had been swept away or ground down to nothing. Sharp edges of the cliffside had been smoothed. Only those of us in the pits had survived.

"Us and the bridge. Mostly. All the wooden braces had vanished. The stone structure remained, though its pillars seemed thinner and—in my eyes—not equal to the task of supporting a cart. I wasn't planning on risking my own body on it. So I wished a farewell to my fellow freed men and women and headed south, toward the distance where the canyon seemed to draw its banks together.

"I have to admit, though, that I regret never seeing that bridge completed. It would have been a fine work." He retreated into reverie for a moment, then shook his head and returned to his tale. "By this time, I was very weak, so it took me several days to trace the canyon to a place where it grew shallower, then to cross it and return to my path through the forest. All that time, the world had fallen silent.

"Almost. A wind was blowing out of the north the day I crossed into the forest, cold but slow. It curled down and lifted wisps of the fine glass back into the trees. The further I went to the west, beyond the path the storm had taken, the more the trees still held their shapes, their branches, their dead autumn leaves. The sparkling breeze brushed across those leaves, a hushing much like the one from the previous night, but quieter, an unending hiss.

"It occurred to me then that it does something warm to my heart to witness things that take much less time to observe than they do to describe. Do you know what I mean?"

Charis nodded, her senses stuck on facing the external, unwilling to wrench them around and examine things inside herself. She set aside the shackles with a dull *clank* and rested her palms on her knees.

"No message could be worth all of this," she said. "None that couldn't be written on paper or hide or magnetic tapes."

The messenger shrugged. "Long, long ago we sent messengers into the skies, beyond the sphere of our knowledge, with very little hope of their messages even being read. I've already achieved more than they ever did, having met you, biovin Charis."

"Still... It seems cruel to send you into the unknown, containing the unknown."

"I volunteered."

Charis studied the messenger's face, trying to imagine how he might have looked before the corruption of his flesh.

"We should probably continue, per the yurchief's request," said the messenger softly, trying not to startle her.

Charis blinked and nodded. "Yes. Can you raise your arms?"

"Partway."

"That will do. The left side, please. I'll be quick."

"Take the time you need. I'm just dying to know what I carry."

Five days passed while Charis worked, recalling her predecessor's instructions and reconditioning the necessary equipment. The messenger spent most of them lying on a cot near her workstation. Charis had sent a watergirl to retrieve the simple bed from her home. The girl had stared goggle-eyed at the messenger until he had given her a little wave, then had darted away. On her return, she had stayed well away from the messenger, unfolding the cot and rushing back toward the door before the messenger could shamble over to it.

"Don't worry," he had said to the girl. "I've not made anyone else sick." The words hadn't sunk in.

Since then, Charis had isolated the helices from the sample from the messenger's lymph tumors and taken two more samples for comparison: one simply from a swab of his cheek, the other from one of the tumors visible near his spine.

For the latter, she had been as careful as possible, and used the last of her sugar cane to deaden his nerves, but still his body had nearly twisted itself off the cot trying to escape the coring needle.

Now, he slept while Charis worked to amplify the fragments of the samples and render them as codes that might contain the message. In her mind, she considered the work backbreaking, because of her habit of bending close to her keyboards and displays and how infrequently she remembered to stretch and relax.

At one point, while waiting for a chemical reaction to complete, Charis felt her eyes drifting closed, and briefly considered taking the speed the yurchief had offered. But she knew what it did to the body, peripheral to the borrowed energy and wakefulness. It was fine for the guard faithful, for the warriors of the vanguard, and for the yurchief himself, but Charis intended to live much longer, much more slowly than any of them.

Gray pre-dawn light was lightening the high windows when the final strand of data resolved on her screens. The software laid the three samples side by side, eliminating the lines of identical data and presenting the differences. She tapped and clicked, reviewing each cut. In every example, the cheek swab showed differences from the two core biopsies where she presumed the message could lie.

But as she laid the data from the tumors side by side, her heart sank.

"Are you making progress?" the messenger asked. He stood a few feet away from her and spoke quietly so as not to startle her.

She bent forward and propped her head in her hands. "Yes and no. The samples from your spine and lymph nodes are significantly different. If there was a message there, it may have been corrupted by one, or by both. Most likely both, since neither is the original. Metastasis may have altered whatever was injected in your liver cells."

The messenger took this in stride, approaching so that he could see the screen over Charis' shoulder. "You have done great work already, my friend," he said. "Do you need my liver?" He said it in the pitch of a joke, but Charis shook her head, answering seriously.

"Even if we take the sample, I'm still confronted by the task of decoding the message it *might* contain. The yurchief will be back in two or three days. These conditions are not... ideal."

The messenger smiled and patted her shoulder and then retreated again to his cot, breathing heavily. The mild exertion of crossing the room seemed to have weakened him.

"Before I volunteered," he began as his lungs caught up to the demand. "Do you know what I was?" Charis shook her head. "I was a poet. I wrote verses on nature and community, real sentimental stuff. Poets are perhaps not necessary to the smooth function of society, but I do believe we are nature's codecs. Do you know that word? We decode the messages of complex systems; we encode the simplicity of life so that it will stick lengthwise in the mind. All messages, to the poet, are in all things."

"That is not a representative view of the world," said Charis.

"It is *precisely* representative. Just not very accurate," said the messenger with a warm chuckle. "I believe in you, Charis. Your successful work does not depend on knowledge you do not possess, nor on effort you are unprepared to undertake. Your only obstacle, I think, is time."

"For us both," said Charis.

The messenger nodded at that and lay back on the cot. "I'm at your disposal," he said.

Charis was silent for a moment. The messenger's breaths began to slow. There was one more piece of information she wanted from him, though. "Why did you volunteer?"

He blew a puff of air out of his nose and rolled to face her, his eyes half-lidded. "I believed there was more to life than poetry. Can you imagine that? Don't answer." The laugh that escaped him was strangely high pitched.

"I don't know much about poetry," said Charis.

"It's all right. I've proven to myself that I don't know much about anything else. It's a truth I've long avoided accepting. When the council asked for volunteers to carry messages to all the scattered tribes, I convinced myself that a humble poet would be the best for this job. All my life, I studied and practiced to draw connections between distant rhetorical points, almost like a soothsayer impressing shapes upon a scattering of stars or a clothier assembling their textures in a beautiful garment. Who better to bear a special missive to strangers than someone trained to draw together the folds of a broad idea and stitch it over a form easy to recognize?"

"Your pride compelled you?"

"My hubris, I would say. It was fueled by decades of feeling underappreciated, I don't mind saying. A poet has one eye forever locked on immortality, but nothing I composed ever would ensure my own. I suppose I felt that, in this effort, I could make a difference. One that might last."

"That was a great risk," said Charis. The messenger didn't offer a disagreement. She went on: "What did you hope you would find at your journey's end?"

The messenger gave the question its due consideration in silence, then, with some effort, shifted onto his back to stare up at the distant, shadowed ceiling. "What I hoped for back then is unimportant. What I hope for now is that I won't die lonely. And that, whatever this message in me turns out to be, it brings people closer together."

Charis looked at her hands. She wondered how many years of life she had preserved among her people, how she might quantify the difference she had made so far. "Perhaps you are the message," she said.

The messenger spluttered a laugh and moved a hand to press against his side. "Oh! Please, my friend. One more puff of conceit into this skull and I fear my head will float away. No, no. There is an end to my life and it has been written in me."

Before Charis' smile had faded, he was asleep.

On the morning of the sixth day since her task had begun, Charis sat and listened to the messenger groaning in his sleep. There was no place and no time where he could escape the pain of his disease. At least he seemed to recover some energy after his naps, despite the apparent discomfort.

Charis left him to his rest and stepped out of the laboratory. The mists of early morning dampened her face and clothes. The air tasted of algae, thick and green. She saw threads of smoke rising above the treetops and could smell cooking meat. A watergirl laced between the nearby trunks, two buckets balanced on a yoke, headed for the laboratory's cistern. Charis caught her eye and nodded to her. In response, the watergirl shook her head and flicked her eyes toward the deeper forest.

Now Charis could hear it: the stamp of heavy feet. An infrequent chime of metal-on-metal suggested the guard faithful. Sure enough, two of them came around a thick fir from the direction of the water. Between them strode the yurchief, back from his hunt ahead of schedule. He had a brace of otters slung over his shoulder and was using his fishing pike as a walking stick, dull end downward.

He nodded when he saw Charis, as if pleased that she had anticipated his coming. "What's the message?" he barked as she drew nearer.

"My apologies, your 'ness," said Charis, bowing her head. "I have not yet retrieved the message."

The yurchief shifted the weight of his kill and sighed. "Look at me."

Charis did as instructed.

"You look exhausted. Did you sleep last night?"

"Not well, your 'ness."

"Did you take my speed?"

"I did not."

The yurchief nodded. He gave a mild gesture with the fingers curled around the pike and both guard faithful relaxed. Charis hadn't even noticed them tensing.

"You still have until tomorrow, upon my original order. I shall leave you to it. But pay attention, biovin. If you fail to deliver the message to me before tomorrow noon, I will consider you a thief: a thief of my time and of what is rightfully mine. You will receive a thief's punishment."

"But, your 'ness," Charis protested. "Without my hands, I would be unable to compound—"

The long pike slammed into the ground hard enough to make the world seem hollow; Charis felt the beat of it rise up in her bones. "You!" The yurchief's voice hit her ears with the same force. "Your value is not in your hands! Your knowledge can be preserved through... much."

"I understand, your 'ness."

"You are burning daylight, biovin."

Charis bowed her head again and left it downturned until the footsteps had gone and the cloying scent of the dead beasts had dissipated. Then she raised her head and let the furious dampness in her eyes intermix with the air's heavy humidity.

When her heart had slowed, she re-entered the laboratory, opening and closing the door as quietly as she could.

She needn't have bothered. The messenger was sitting up on the cot, half-propped against the wall.

"You need more rest," said Charis.

"I don't," said the messenger. "It takes hours to process a sample, yes? We had better get started."

"I'm out of sugar cane."

"It won't matter, Charis." He levered himself off the cot and approached her. "He would really take your hands?"

"It's the punishment for thieves."

"Some would rather choose exile, I imagine."

"There is no exile. Nothing is beyond the yurchief."

"Come now," said the messenger. His expression shuddered for a moment and then went still, as if he lacked the energy to shift it to any purpose. His voice settled into a warm valley, though. "There is much beyond the yurchief."

Charis let her gaze fall to the biopsy needle. It hadn't gone through the autoclave since its last use. She feared there wouldn't now be enough time. "I might kill you," she said.

The messenger sighed and sat down on the creaking office chair. "I don't believe you'll have the chance, my friend. You could, of course, wait until after I am gone, but would you deny me at least the chance to see the unknown inside me? Come now. It'll be over quicker than I could write it down."

Charis looked at her hands, gray in the thin light, and flexed her fingers. They held steady. She nodded. "But give me a moment." She touched his shoulder, noting the quiver in his body that he seemed unable to still. Then she went and retrieved a portion of the yurchief's speed. She dug through the ingredients in her refrigerator and added careful measures of several to the drug, then diluted the mixture in water. She brought a beakerful to the messenger's lips. "Drink."

He obeyed, licking his lips afterward. "If I see eternity, I intend to keep far away," he said, rumbling a laugh that devolved into a coughing fit. Charis helped him from the chair onto one of the benches, laying him out beneath the strongest light. His eyes closed as the high took hold and he made barely a whimper when the needle punctured his abdomen.

The sun had been rising for hours before its light found Charis through the high lab windows, head bent, muscles giving up any hope of relief. By mid-morning, the cut segments of the liver sample were rendering on her display. She began to compare them to the other three, noting strings of differences, eliminating common patterns. On and on.

The symbols assigned to each piece of data began to blur together. Charis rubbed her eyes and looked up at the high windows. The branches of the trees were still, as if making an effort not to disturb her. The only sound in the room came from the hum of fans and the labored breathing of the messenger.

I could live in exile, thought Charis. *If there are lands beyond the yurchief, beyond the Mallers. I could go to the Calomlands.* She had never been beyond the Sound, had never even had to spend a night beneath the stars. *Would I have volunteered?* She had no answer for herself. Absently, she cracked her knuckles and regretted it at once as the messenger stirred.

He opened one eye and fixed it on her. The color had left his skin, his tumors ashen gray and the porous skin in the clefts between them fully white.

"How is it going?" he asked.

Charis left her work and came to kneel at his side. "Not well," she said. She calmed her voice by speaking like a biovin. "The sequences were well-extracted, but I still cannot locate the message, and even if I were to locate it now, I don't believe I could decrypt it in time. I've been giving it some thought, and since the cipher must be more complex than simple substitution, compressing our alphabet into the limited set of—" She stopped herself abruptly, the absence of the words permitting a lump to rise in her throat.

Her hands sought out his and together they held some warmth in stasis.

"I don't think I can do it," she said.

"Charis, Charis," said the messenger. "What a gift it has been to find someone who might read the messages in me—" His eyes fluttered. "Oh, eternity," he whispered, unable to focus on anything close at hand. Charis squeezed his fingers and he returned for a moment. "We are drawn together across a great distance.

Do you see it?" He forced a smile onto lips unwilling to cooperate.

His heartbeat slackened, then, and stopped.

Charis tightened her grip on his hands, relaxed, then tightened again, repeating the motion over and over, as if she could urge his pulse to return. It took some time for the absurdity to penetrate her conscious mind.

Finally she stood and left him alone. She trailed her fingers over the equipment on her table, let them brush over the keyboards and controls. Who knew what accidental changes her careless touch might have made to her work? She snapped off the power. In the silence that followed, a clicking came from the high windows. Pine needles tapped against the glass.

Charis went outside, leaving the laboratory door open behind her. A breeze was beginning to stir in the forest.

One of the watergirls, headed past on her way to the cistern, noticed her standing there and approached hesitantly.

"Miss, are you alright?"

It took Charis a great effort to fix her attention on the girl, as if the thickness of the air resisted the motion of her eyes. *No,*

Charis corrected herself, ever searching for precision, because it wasn't the world beyond her flesh that slowed her; it was the atmosphere within, the swirl of her intentions anchored at some midpoint she couldn't visualize. Words wouldn't come out.

"Did you find the message, biovin?" The watergirl's voice carried a lilt of excitement.

Charis turned her attention again to the trees. That riot of thoughts within her spun on and on and she realized that, though they all were tied to the eye at the center, that eye was in motion. Charis recalled the messenger's cold skin.

"Biovin?" The watergirl now seemed to be getting worried, leaning in closer.

Charis let her lips fall apart and pulled in rushing air between them. "Would you," she began, pausing as the words went out and did not return. "Would you like to learn the work of a biovin? I could teach you everything I know."

"I'm sorry?"

"And maybe I will be a poet."

The branches around them gently scraped the air, hissing. It was an inconstant sound, inward and outward, as if driven by breaths drawn and exhaled.

No, Charis chided herself. *A slackening moment like this should take much less time to describe than to observe.*

The wind moved in the trees.

The yurchief received Charis in his audience hall, a stone-and-thatch longhouse with three fires spaced equidistant down the length. Each fire was stoked fiercely hot, but directed mainly upward, so that as she crossed the distance from the entrance to the wooden throne her skin alternately blazed feverish and chilled beneath her damp sweat. Her mind echoed the pattern as she rehearsed what she might say, in turns raging with anger and then withdrawing to cold darkness.

As she bowed, she felt the stresses of the differentials might crack her down the middle, but in fact only her voice did as she made her decision and said, "Your 'ness, I have your message."

The yurchief looked down at her. He leaned back in his throne, the wooden joints creaking. The thick air made it hard to see his expression. Charis blinked and wiped at her face, feeling for an irrational moment that her eyes had been darkened like smoked glass.

She sensed he was waiting for her to go on. She took a deep breath. The words came to her mind barely before they left her tongue, and they quavered as they went.

"The message is a simple text of friendship, your 'ness, extended by the councilors of the Calomlands. They wish prosperity upon you and your people and invite us to reply by any means." The lie mingled easily with the grime suspended in the air between them. Charis bowed again, willing her shaking knees to calm. "They indicated landmarks for navigation to their homelands," she added, hoping that the messenger's story would supply enough detail if pressed.

"Friendship," said the yurchief, the word curling out of his mouth like smoke.

Charis nodded, fixing her attention on a whorl in the pattern of the stone floor, an image like the eye of a storm.

"Worthless. Leave us," the yurchief barked to those at his side. "You stay, biovin." A shuffling of footsteps around them told Charis that the various guard faithful and soothsayers were filing to the exit. Her flesh ignited and then froze.

"You are telling me the truth," the yurchief muttered, leaden tone absorbing all inflection if it had been a question.

"Yes, your 'ness," said Charis. *All messages are in all things.* She repeated the messenger's words to herself. It did little to bring about an equilibrium.

"Look at me," the yurchief said. Charis obeyed. "The tribe is glad for your skills," he went on. "They are a tribute to us all. Well done." A pressure wave of relief built up inside her. "Tell me, exactly: how did they address me?"

"The message was addressed to whomever leads the people," said Charis.

The yurchief snorted a laugh and rose. He clasped his hands behind his back, ambling past Charis to just within the corona of the nearest fire. He stretched out his hands to warm them and then nodded for her to join him.

"It would only be proper to compose a reply, don't you think?"

"Yes, your 'ness." She stopped herself before asking if he intended her to carry the response. The relief had faltered and dissipated.

"Entertain me, biovin. What would you say to such a message?"

"I would respond in kind. Offer our friendship. Perhaps, in the future, we might have an exchange of knowledge and equipment."

"It would not be swift enough, I'm afraid, biovin. While you have been stuck to your workbench, the world beyond you has been changing. There have been storms along our borders, brutal ones which leave nothing behind. They're coming closer. Soon, they will scour the Sound to its barren bones. We must be away from here before that happens."

"Storms of glass?" asked Charis. The yurchief nodded, turning a curious gaze on her until she explained: "The messenger witnessed such a thing near the end of his journey."

The yurchief shrugged. "Then perhaps the Calomlands are safe from them, as yet." He let his eyes drift over the flames. "They were my home, once," he said, far away. "Plains of green grass. Lakes full of fish and forests full of game. But I'm afraid my mind was not so narrow as they would have liked."

Shocked, Charis made a sound like an apology, inconsequential. The yurchief crossed his thick arms and closed himself down, eyes and all.

"Where is your gratitude to me, I wonder?" he said. "With my own strength, I have ensured our survival. I put those lands behind me, with their conceited council and the preening philosophers in their alabaster domes. This gray lump in my skull was a pitiful thing, in their consideration, and my destiny was set as a sludge-man, an offal-bearer.

"*You* would be accepted, of course, in no time at all, biovin Charis. Their sole pride was in the supremacy of their minds. They do not and would not have the strength to survive, to *thrive* as we have here in the Sound."

Silence expanded in time and space, filling the seconds and the rafters.

"Friendship, you swear?" The yurchief's throat rasped with phlegm. He spat into the fire. "There's no ambiguity in the message?"

Charis quailed, but any deviation from the message would surely bring the whole thing to an end. "There is no ambiguity."

The yurchief chuckled. "Then I know what I shall say. And I will etch my words in stone, where they might be read by anyone. And the host of us will follow just behind the messenger. We will cross the lands, ahead of the storms. They expect friendship, but they did not know who would read their message. I will return at the prow of war. You are dismissed, biovin."

He turned to face the fire and spat again. As he lowered his head, his hair fell away from his neck. Charis blinked and stared. A cyst had been exposed there, small, pale, but casting a large and dancing shadow. She opened her mouth and found no words for a long moment.

"Yes, your 'ness," she said finally.

Charis returned to the laboratory in silence and worry. Once inside, with the door closed, she disrobed. The cool of the evening and the threat of rain drew gooseflesh all over her skin. She examined her body in a mirror but found no lesions, no evidence of illness. Afterward, satisfied for the time being, she wrapped herself in layers and sat in front of the messenger's body for a long while.

There was so much she didn't know. She realized how desperately she wanted to confess just that to the messenger, to hear him offer his interpretation of her words and her world. *If I were smarter, or faster, or had better tools*, she thought, but silenced the voice inside before reaching a conclusion.

Being there, in the unknowing, was not unusual for her. It was part of the job of the biovin to learn, to build small answers upon each other until they reached a larger one. But for the first time in her work, she felt tormented by the blank void of unanswered questions, questions which *could not* be answered. At least, not there in the laboratory nestled in the Sound.

If the yurchief truly intended to lead his people to the Calomlands, it would take time for him to assemble them all. There would be bustle and confusion and little for Charis to contribute unless he ran out of his speed, now that he believed he had his message and his purpose.

If there are answers for me, she thought, *they are beyond his reach. Now and maybe forever.* She could slip away in the night and be ahead of the vanguard by days, turning to weeks if his condition followed the course of the messenger's. She could reach the Calomlands, a little storm of her own, full of swirling questions and fears and warnings.

Or perhaps the glass storms will sweep through and scour the lands clean of all our complexities, our imperfections.

The decision rose in her like a sudden gust. She filled a satchel with medicines that would travel well, and retrieved a stash of dried meat and nuts. Almost as an afterthought, she crammed the hard copies of the data extracted from the messenger alongside the provisions. When she stepped out into the evening, the damp wind hit what little skin she had left exposed like a bloody lash. She turned her back against it and set out for the Eastern path. Her path would take her through the drying forest, over the mountains, over the plains, to the Calomlands, bearing with her the unknown and the unknowable, and the hope of crossing bridges to meet those who might help her find the soul of the message inside her.

See Ian Donnell Arbuckle's story "The Hissing Trees" online at Metaphorosis.
If you liked it, leave a comment. Authors love that!
Remember to subscribe to our e-mail updates so you'll know when new stories are posted.

About the story

This story is the product of a couple of characters bouncing around from different story stubs until they found each other. The messenger was originally the protagonist of an unfinished novel a few years back, which was focused on the delivery of secret messages through manipulation of the messengers' genes. The character of Charis, in "The Hissing Trees", started out as a bit player in a different post-apocalyptic story, where her pragmatism was a foil for the narrator's irritating optimism. Neither of the characters ended up following the arcs I had envisioned, so those projects languished. A few years back, the University of Washington publicized some efforts they had made to store data in DNA (www.washington.edu/news/2016/04/07/uw-team-stores-digital-images-in-dna-and-retrieves-them-perfectly) and it sparked my imagination enough to get a basic outline down in my writing journal, but it took several years before I tried fitting the two characters together with the key decision not to bother with giving away the actual message hidden in the messenger. This fouled up Charis' personal commitment to her scientific method and removed the messenger's full involvement with the mission he was on, and I had my story about confronting the unknown, and finding those with whom you can reluctantly accept your ignorance.

A question for the author

Q: What's easier for you — imagining a happier world, or a darker one?

A: It's much easier for me to imagine a darker world. I think that's for a couple of reasons. For one, I have depression and anxiety and my brain is somewhat predisposed to see the negatives in things. But it's also more interesting for me, as a writer, to imagine dark worlds because their conflicts provide the necessary soil to nourish a story. I suppose a happy world isn't necessarily free of conflict, but I'll confess that my ideal has less of it. So, imagining a darker world is easier, but when it comes to putting in the work, I'll gladly make the effort to bring about a happier one.

About the author

Ian Donnell Arbuckle lives deep in the desert half of Washington State with his wife and children.

@IanArbuckle1

The Crystal Pyramid

Mia Ram

There's not a soul in this city-state who hasn't heard of the Crystal Pyramid. It is the lost wonder of the ancient world, the point where the lines between history and legend blur. Countless scholars, writers, and artists have imagined how it must have looked.

I do not need to imagine. I have seen it with my own eyes.

I remember it stood lonely among the pale dunes, its every edge sharpened to perfection, its crystalline facade so pure it reflected the sun's rays back to the sky. Was it the most beautiful thing I had ever seen? Perhaps, but given the circumstances, that was no shining endorsement. I had just travelled across hundreds of leagues, riding through nothing but sand wastes. I had sailed the malicious seas that churned between our continent and theirs. I had dragged myself across a desolate land with no one but my horse for company. After all that, even a rotting shack would have looked beautiful to me.

"Take a whiff of the air, Fig." I patted my horse's neck as she trotted toward the pyramid. "You know what that smell is?"

Fig whinnied.

"Success, Fig. It's the smell of success." I rode her to the very edge of the pyramid before bringing her to a stop and swinging off of her. "Well, there's nowhere to stable you. But you're not going to be stupid and run off, are you?"

Fig huffed.

"Smart girl. You just wait here for me until I find the entrance for us, and when all this is over, I'll give you all the lettuce you can eat." I grabbed my satchel off her saddle and slung it over my shoulder, then shot her a final salute. "Wish me luck, whatever that's worth. We're about to be very rich, Fig. Very rich."

Granted, I was already very rich by that point. But I wasn't the *richest*. And the sun is not content to rise only halfway up the sky.

I began as a little wailing nobody, born to another nobody beneath a nameless bridge in the city-state of Summer's Edge. My mother believed in playing life's game fair, and little good it did us living as street rats. Ours was a life of barely enough. Barely enough to eat and drink. Barely enough shelter, barely enough clothing, barely enough to exist.

Then she died. In the cold of that first night alone in the gutter, I asked myself questions. What would it be like to have more than just barely enough? What would it be like to not have to slave and beg for scraps, to simply *take* what you want?

To leave uncrackable vaults empty. To con the sharpest merchants out of every coin. To fill coffer after coffer, eventually with enough to buy my way into the aristocratic circles.

What would it be like to have everything?

I discovered it was like flying.

The greatest of flights began a few months before I arrived at the Crystal Pyramid, in a narghile lounge in the gold district. I'd been invited there by an old friend. Akeem was a fellow thief turned merchant, one who had also played the game well enough to climb from the low streets to the high towers of the city-state. We had run more than a few cons and thefts together. A childhood disease had left him unable to use his legs, so he'd relied on mine to sneak into wealthy windows or through crowded markets, just as I relied on his lightning wit to craft escape routes and elaborate frauds when my own wouldn't do. He was the only person I'd met since my mother that I trusted.

The lounge was spread across the roof of the district's highest tower, all satin cushions and rugs imported from island states to the south. Even the narghile supplied to me was ringed with rubies along the base. They were poorly set in the gold, though. I was able to chip them all off and slip them into my pockets before Akeem even joined me on the sofa. I watched his attendants carry him in on a silver palanquin, then help him onto the seat across from me.

"Thank you. Wait for me below," he told them, shooing them away. Once they'd left us, he turned his attention back to me. "And thank you for meeting me here, Bazi."

I blew some smoke aside and shrugged. "You ought to be thankful. I'm rarely this generous with my time. I'm a busy woman."

"But never too busy for a smoke with a good friend, surely?" Akeem smiled.

"Not when I've only got the one," I said with a wink. "But really, this better be good. I've got plans that need attending to."

"So the rumors say. I can't go down two streets in the rich districts without hearing something about you. Rather surprising things."

"You ought to know better than to pay any mind to rumors about me. Half of those are merely venomous lies spread by the many who envy my fortune. And my talent, wit, and beauty. Why, it's no wonder I have enemies." I grinned and tried to keep my tone light-hearted. "Let's not waste time. What's this proposal you wanted me to hear?"

"Well, that has to do somewhat with rumors as well. They say you've aspirations toward the royal families," said Akeem, drumming his fingers on his knee.

"Do they, now?" My grin tightened. Akeem shouldn't have known that, especially not second-hand. It's much harder to slip your way into a circle once everyone knows you're trying to get in. It must have been that damn Naji, my lover at the time, running his mouth around the pleasure district. Some men you can't tell anything.

Akeem grabbed the pipe from my hand and took a leisurely inhale. "As esteemed as you've become, Bazi, you must realize that such a thing would be nigh impossible for you. Even the richest merchant would never be considered for marriage into one of the seven royal families."

"Nothing is impossible for me." I snatched the pipe back. "And I certainly need no advice on the matter from you. What do you know of the royal families, anyway?"

"In general? Not more than expected. Of Prince Sef in particular? Quite a bit."

I froze. "Prince Sef? Of the Dram family?"

Akeem's grin widened. "Ah, now I have your attention."

I fought to keep myself collected. Sef's family was the oldest in Summer's Edge, its founding family. As the eldest, he stood to become the most powerful, wealthiest person in the city-state. Along with whatever woman could manage to marry him.

Akeem leaned in, his eyes alight. "I happen to have befriended the prince's former tutor at this very lounge, mere months ago. After a few drinks, he told me that Prince Sef has long been seized by an obsession with the history of the Empire of Heaven, as well as its last empress, Eru. And her tomb, the Crystal Pyramid. Do you know what they say she was buried with? Enchanted automatons, wax wings that flew, and even a pair of lenses that would allow the wearer to see the future."

"Magic lenses, hm?" I laughed at the thought. "Oh, the things I could do with that."

"Legend says these are but a few of her treasures, and the prince would give his arm for even one of them. Any woman who could bring back a relic for him would win his heart enough to overcome his feelings on status and blood."

"All well and good if I could ever find such a thing," I scoffed.

Akeem held up a hand to silence me. He turned to the satchel beside him and pulled bundles of papers and books out from his satchel, selecting one sheet to hand to me. I took it and stared down at the world in ink. I traced one of the routes with my finger, eyes going wide.

"This isn't our continent."

"Indeed not. It is the one that lies across the Carmelian Seas. Few have even voyaged to its shores, much less traversed it."

"*That's* what this is?" I snapped, though I couldn't tear my eyes from the map. "Of course few voyage there. Even I've heard how dangerous the Carmelian seas are, and those who've survived say nothing lies on the other side but sand."

"Sand, and the ruins of the lost Empire." Akeem kept his eyes steady on mine. There was no mirth there, no hint of a jest at my expense. "I can trust no one else with this, Bazi. I've reached across the farthest, most shadowed corners of the continent for the information you now hold in your hands. What lies within the Crystal Pyramid could make us both rich beyond our wildest dreams. I can provide the ship, the supplies, everything you could need for the expedition. The only thing I cannot do is sail myself. I need you."

And so there I was months later, my expedition guided by the maps and texts from Akeem. The theoretical inventory of Empress Eru's burial chamber was admittedly the least useful, but I couldn't seem to help myself from reading it constantly, imagining those treasures as I journeyed to a forgotten land. It was a comfort through the tempests that rocked my ship, and on the endless nights when the dunes went cold. I clutched it close to my heart when the worst of the thirst hit and the only oasis near was a mirage. I traced its letters when the sandstorms kept Fig and me trapped in my tent for days. Through all these torments, the promise of the burial chamber was my only comfort. And always, I dreamed of the magic lenses. Surely there wasn't a problem in the world that couldn't be solved with them. Like the problem of the door.

"This is madness, Fig," I told the horse on my third circuit around the pyramid's perimeter. "There has to be a way in. Damn me to Hells, I should have just brought along some explosives. Just take out this wall right here, and the trouble would be over with!"

I rifled through the tools I'd brought in my satchel, hoping that perhaps I had packed something combustive and somehow forgot. No such luck. The closest thing to useful was my hammer, one of few tools I had packed, but even that barely managed to penetrate the crystal wall when I tested it.

Fig whinnied behind me and tilted her ear. She beat her hoof against the sand.

"Oh, quit your whining, spoiled beast," I snapped at her. "You haven't been waiting long."

Fig paid me no mind. She whinnied again and broke into a trot around to the other side of the pyramid. I ran after her, hurling every curse in existence at her as I did.

"Fig, there's no room in the Heavens for ungrateful curs!" I yelled as she slowed to a stop by the pyramid's north-facing wall.

I caught up and wagged my finger in her face. "If you think for one second that this is acceptable behavior—"

I paused as a ringing sounded behind me. I turned, stunned to find that the walls of the pyramid were slowly parting behind me to reveal a mirror twice my size and height.

"—then you are absolutely correct. Well done, Fig." I patted Fig's neck and stared at my reflection. Hopeful that the mirror functioned as a door, I tried pushing against it with my full weight. It didn't budge an inch. I was about to ram myself against it again when I saw something faint in the mirror, superimposed over my reflection. I pressed my face to the glass and squinted. On the other side stood a silver lion.

He stepped closer to the glass. "Name yourself, strange traveler."

"What in the name of all Hells!" I stared at the creature, stunned to my core. I had seen many oddities in my day, but a talking lion was a first. "What are you?"

"I am Malak," Malak answered, baring his fangs. "Imperial messenger and guard, bidden to deny entry to the unworthy. As you must be if you lack even the faculties to identify yourself."

"I'm Bazi."

"Of what House?"

I shrugged. "I need no house or distinguished blood. I was born beneath a bridge in Summer's Edge and found it to be a perfectly fine starting place."

"Well, Bazi of the Bridge, if it is entry to the Empress' chamber you seek, you must prove yourself."

"Well, isn't that how it always goes. Straight out of a fairytale," I snorted. "Are you about to present me with some twisty riddle?"

Malak paused for a moment before answering. "You are already familiar with the trials of the Pyramid?"

"Call it an educated guess," I said. "Let's hear it. I didn't get to where I am by being stupid. I'll make quick work of whatever riddle you have."

Malak nodded. "Very well. Who is the one who drinks yet is ever thirsty, eats yet always hungers, who walks in shadows through every door and window, and shall inherit the world with a sleight of hand?"

I stared blankly for a moment, the words dancing about in my head as I tried to make sense of them. Always thirsty? Walks in shadows? I thought for another moment before the answer became clear.

"It's all nonsense!" I declared. "There is no true answer, the riddle only exists to waste time and confuse the listener. I see right through it."

"No, there is a single true answer—" Malak began, but I waved a hand to shush him.

"Of course not. If there was, I would have thought of it already. I'm sure that false riddle has turned others from your door, but such tricks won't work on a sharper wit, Kitten." I opened my satchel and dug until I found what I required. "Hah! Let's try this beauty again."

"Just what do you think you're doing?" Malak's eyes widened as I struck the mirror with my hammer and began to fracture its surface.

"Exactly what it looks like."

"This is not how things are done!" Malak snarled through the glass.

"It is now!" I gritted my teeth. Each strike against the glass took all my strength, to my amazement. This same hammer had blasted my way through dozens of windows with ease, yet the glass of the mirror seemed as difficult to break as iron.

"You're not even going to *attempt* to answer?"

"I already told you, if there were a clear answer, I'd have thought of it. I won't lose hours playing your little game. I've already lost months just to get here," I said as I continued to fight against the glass. "I've starved, nearly been blown overboard and drowned, and wandered the desert for leagues. You want a damn answer? Here it is!"

The mirror shattered. One swift kick and the glass rained down on the other side.

I stepped inside. "There we are!"

Malak beat his paw on the ground. "That is not how this is intended to proceed! You've ruined the entrance. I was not designed to repair broken doors."

"Designed?" With the mirror gone and the blue glow of the lanterns lining the walls, I could see Malak clearly. The silver was not of fur but actual metal, his dark eyes were marble stones, and the gears within his body could be heard with his every move. An automaton.

I poked him with the hammer. "What an odd specimen you are! I've half a mind to take *you* apart, see what makes you tick, then build copies to sell in the market square."

"Try that and I'll take you apart!" Malak snarled. "What are you doing?"

"I don't suppose you have a stable around here?" I asked after I whistled my horse over. I swept the stray glass aside with my foot as Fig gingerly stepped through the gaping mirror, which was just wide enough for her to fit through. "No? No matter, she can wait here."

"This is the Crystal Pyramid, not a horse stable."

"Seems like you've plenty of room for her anyhow." I looked around at the vast, empty floor until I saw a grand stairwell on the other side of the level. "Now, on we go."

Malak sulked by my heels as we ascended to the second level of the Pyramid, clearly displeased at having been outwitted by me. He grumbled about fate and worthiness, but I couldn't be bothered to listen. Far grander things occupied my mind. For, if Akeem had been right about an enchanted automaton, what other artifacts of legend lay hidden in the Pyramid? I thought again of the magic lenses. With a view into the future, anything could be within my grasp.

"Tell me, my feline friend, what sort of treasures did that Empress of yours lock with her in her burial chamber?" I asked Malak.

"Of what concern is that to you?"

"Oh, mere curiosity."

Malak huffed, his marble eyes rolling my way. "It sounds as if you are thinking of taking something from Her Majesty's chamber."

"Why, never! I'm only a humble explorer, Kitten." I stopped short as we finally reached the top step. Just ahead was a wide entryway that split into multiple paths, one to the right, one straight onward, and one to the left. "What's this? A maze?"

"Yes." Malak nodded. "This trial is intended to test your patience and memory."

"Believe me, my patience has more than been tested," I said. I stared at the entrances a moment, tapping my foot as I thought. "Hm."

"Begin from any point," said Malak. He stood and watched beside the left-most wall.

I turned to him, an idea forming. Any point, eh?

I quickly jumped up on his back before he could move out from under my feet.

"What are you doing?" Malak snapped.

"Just stay still a moment," I replied. I reached to grasp the top of the maze wall and hauled myself to the edge. High above me was the ceiling, its shine heightened by the legions of lanterns lining the maze walls. From here, I could see the entire maze stretching all the way to the other end of the room, where the next stairwell waited. I considered walking the walltops, but given their relatively slim width, I figured the balancing act it would require would waste more time than it would save. From my satchel, I grabbed one of the maps and a worn charcoal stick. I proceeded to sketch a rough map of the maze on the back, as well as outline the path that led to its exit. It was quite an easy maze to solve when seen from above. Amateur, even.

"This is not how the puzzle is meant to be solved!" Malak called up at me. "Have you no concern for honor or integrity?"

"Honor and integrity never awarded anyone riches," I said curtly. "Honor and integrity are fine things to have when you're already born with your every need and desire met, but when you're born destitute beneath a bridge, you cannot afford such childish ideals."

"You need not sacrifice those 'childish ideals', as you call them, to improve your station in life." Malak growled. "Have you even tried?"

"Have you?" I snapped back at him, and naturally, he had no reply. "My mother did. All it earned her was a knife in her back, and her final moments wasted in the dark of an alleyway. Her blood still stains my nightmares. It was a city guard that did it. Honest work for honest pay, he told her, until she dared to ask for the pay. If she'd have just stolen it off him, she'd still be breathing."

"And so now you steal?"

"To thrive. I have as much of a right to do that as those born to golden cribs. Don't you see? Life her way was misery and boredom. Life my way is endless thrills, luxury, and adventure. Taking what I want has set me free." I winked down at him.

"Greed is its own chain," he replied.

"I'll tell you the same thing I told myself on my first night as an orphan, Malak: I'll never have a knife in my back. I'll never live and die in the dark of an alleyway. I'll live in the palace towers, where nothing can touch me, where I can take whatever I want. Only that will be enough."

I finished my map and lowered myself back down to the ground as gently as I could manage.

I nodded to Malak. "Keep up, Kitten."

Malak was silent for half of our journey through the maze, likely bitter that I had outwitted the rules once more, but that didn't bother me. I was eager to make my way to the next level and waste as little time as possible. Had I not been in a rush, I would have spent more time looking at the walls. Beautifully detailed scenes had been engraved on each one. There were scenes of coronations, battles, and rituals. As I passed through, I saw the portraits of what must have been Empresses past, halos glowing around their stately heads. Put together, it all seemed to tell a story, though I couldn't parse what the story was.

"What are all these things engraved around us?" I asked Malak.

"Scenes of the Empire's history," he said. "Had you solved the puzzle properly, you would have recognized each as a historical event, tracing your way from the rise to the fall."

"Well, that would have been impossible," I said, idly running my fingers along the scenes. "There's not enough known about the Empire now to reconstruct all its history."

"Nonsense! The Empire of Heaven was the greatest in the world," Malak growled.

"A few thousand years ago, sure. But now it's buried in the sand wastes and mostly lost to history."

Malak glared at me. "I suppose I shouldn't be surprised. Your ancestors were poor record keepers and near-savages. They could not comprehend the glory of the Empire. Have you heard of Dassin the Sunborn?"

"How would I? I'm a near-savage," I drawled.

"She was a genius sorceress descended from the sun goddess. She conquered this unruly continent and built it into a paradise. She poured her plundered riches into observatories, alchemical forges, and universities."

"Wonderful, Dassin!" I clapped wildly before stopping to cup my hand to my ear. "But what was that word I just heard?

'Plundered'? Weren't you yapping earlier about 'honor' and 'integrity'?"

"That is not the same," said Malak. "Empress Dassin did what was necessary for the greatness of the Empire."

"Greatness, is it?" I snorted.

"Yes. To look beyond your own fleeting, material needs, to reach for the height of what you could become and of the change you could create."

"My material needs aren't fleeting."

Malak bared his fangs, the metal of his muzzle grinding as it lifted. "You would not joke if you understood what was lost. We had no sickness, no hunger, no pain. Every house was a palace, every fountain overflowing with crystal waters, every garden singing. We could project pictures across the Empire with the blink of an eye. Our automaton horses outran the wind. Our cities pierced the clouds. We could *fly*."

I raised an eyebrow. "If you say so, Kitten. But, if your empire was capable of all that, how did it fall?"

Malak went silent. I would have pressed him further, but by then we were at the maze's end, and the next stairwell awaited.

"I'm impressed, Malak. This is the creepiest thing I have ever seen."

I stood at the entrance of the third level with hundreds of marble eyes staring at me. The shining white figures filled the pavilion. Every statue was a flawless replica of a person. Every human of every stripe was present, from soldiers to princesses, to butchers, to scholars. It was as though an entire village had been gathered there and frozen in time.

"There's got to be hundreds of these," I said.

"Yes, but you need only one." Malak lifted his paw and pointed toward the center of the pavilion. Peppered across the pavilion were unoccupied tiles of every color and shade. "The trial is simple. Move the correct statue to that crimson tile in the center left, and the door shall unlock."

"How can I possibly guess which statue is the correct one?"

"Look down and work from there."

I looked down and realized that words were engraved on the tile. Indeed, all the tiles across the pavilion were host to either brief sentences or people's names. I stepped back to read the words on which I'd been standing.

WHO IS THE ONE WHO

I grinned. "It's the first words to that silly little riddle of yours. I only need to find the next line, correct?"

Malak said nothing, but I knew I was right. It was the only solution that made sense. Luckily the riddle was still fresh in my mind. I looked around at all the surrounding tiles until I finally spotted the next line a few steps away.

DRINKS YET IS EVER THIRSTY

"I don't even have to get creative this time," I called over to Malak with a laugh. "This is ludicrously easy!"

About seven steps to the right was the tile with the next line.

EATS YET ALWAYS HUNGERS

"I would have thought that the *greatest empire* would at least know how to craft a challenging puzzle. You ought to let me design the next Crystal Pyramid." Another tile five steps ahead.

WHO WALKS IN SHADOWS

"Even my dimwitted Naji could solve this." The next tile was a mere two steps to the left.

THROUGH EVERY DOOR AND WINDOW

"I hope the burial chamber lives up to the legends. Wouldn't want to have gone through all this for some vases. Ah, there's the next one."

AND SHALL INHERIT THE WORLD

"You're dead quiet, Malak. Cat got your —" I stopped short as I stepped on the final tile.

WITH A SLEIGHT OF HAND?

I stared at the statue that stood before me, her face pulled back in a wry grin, a satchel slung over her shoulder, and her boots dusty from a journey to a forgotten desert. At her feet were two words.

THE THIEF.

I stumbled backward from the statue of myself, a soft gasp escaping my lips. It was so detailed in its carving that I half expected it to reach out and grab me.

"Malak, what is this?" My voice broke as I spoke. I turned my head to find Malak padding toward me.

He tilted his head. "The answer to the riddle."

I turned again to stare at my statue, utterly shaken. How could *I* be the answer to a riddle crafted before my birth?

I then noticed the faces of the statues standing behind it. To the left, a marble replica of Naji. To the right, Akeem. Behind them, my mother.

Malak nudged me with his nose. "All that's left is to move the piece to the red tile that bears your name."

"No! I demand an explanation, immediately!" I told him, but he was already padding away to the door. "How does this thing have *my* face? Why do you have copies of Naji, and my mother? *Answer me!*"

Malak didn't. He merely waited by the door at the pavilion's edge.

Again I looked at my double. A psychological test, designed to break me. It nearly did. Every fiber of my body screamed to turn and run, to hop on Fig and never look back.

But I had come this far. If this did allow me entry to the chamber and its treasures, all that I had ever wanted could finally be mine.

I braced myself against the statue and slid it to the red tile that bore my name. As the tile sank beneath the statue's weight, a click echoed through the pavilion. The door was open.

The stairwell to the burial chamber was the highest yet. The easy confidence with which I'd ascended the lower levels had evaporated now, supplanted by a quiet, creeping dread. I was half certain that cursed statue was following behind, laughing silently with my every step.

The door at the top was open, a pale glow reaching out of it and cascading down the steps ahead of me. It grew brighter the higher I climbed. It was like walking up to a star, dread intermingling with wonder, knowing with each step that I was reaching for something that wasn't meant for human touch.

Finally, I was at the door. I blinked against the siren light and stepped into the Empress' burial chamber.

Three of the walls were translucent, so that I could see all of the desert stretched out before me, even the sand-worn peaks of smaller pyramids, buried by the ages. The fourth wall was thicker than the others, opaque and cool to the touch. When I peered into it, I saw the barest outlines of a woman frozen with her arms across her chest. The Empress in endless sleep.

Within these walls were coffers overflowing with gems of every cut and color, robes of silk woven from clouds, and golden coins minted with ancient visages. There were six of Malak's automaton kin standing guard at the corners, though they were not lions. Among them were a giant eagle, an ox, and even a human, all in silver. He wore the wax wings that Akeem had spoken of, pressed against his back. There were crystals that could summon moving images from the air, a mirror that spoke, and clocks that tracked the cycles of the moon and planets. Everywhere I looked, another marvel awaited.

It'll take a fleet of ships to take this all back to Summer's Edge, I thought to myself.

Naturally, I first targeted the jewels.

Malak was nowhere in sight, and the other automatons neither moved nor spoke as I spirited away every precious thing I could into my satchel. All the dread and fear from the pavilion flew from me as my satchel grew heavier. A few of the most valuable things I had to save for Akeem, as per our agreement, but the rest was all for me.

I grabbed a ruby-ringed crown from the top of one of the coffers, swinging it around my finger. *My wedding gift for you, Prince Sef.*

"You seem to have made yourself quite at home, Bazi of the Bridge."

I jumped at Malak's voice, nearly dropping the crown. "Kitten! I hope you don't mind me nosing about. I couldn't contain my curiosity."

"Explore to your heart's content." Malak padded closer. "You have passed the trials. All that you see here is yours."

"What? Truly?" A smile lit my face, and I crammed the crown into my satchel. "Well, that makes this all easier. I intend to return with a caravan of wagons, once

I've secured the ships and crew. I was also going to hire some mercenaries in case … well, perhaps I'll hire some regardless, to ward off thieves on the journey back. What of these automatons? Can they walk alongside my horse to the eastern shoreline, where my ship waits? I'll require servants once I've—"

"You'll have to convince them yourself once they reawaken," said Malak. He looked at me with a tilted gaze. "I notice you've filled your bag with all manner of gems and gadgets, yet neglected the single treasure I would have thought would most intrigue you. It is the only thing in this chamber that cannot be found anywhere else in the world. Handed down to Empress Eru by the gods themselves."

"The gods themselves?" I asked softly.

Malak nodded to a pedestal that stood before the opaque wall. On it was a small, wooden box, so plain that my eyes had passed it over before.

I walked over to it and cracked open the lid. Inside were a pair of lenses. I lifted them into the light, breathless. They were not a typical pair of transparent lenses. They were round prisms, with each sparkling facet changing color with the light, and were held in place with a golden frame.

I turned to Malak. "Are these what I think they are? The lenses that tell the future?"

"It is not as simple as that, I'm afraid," said Malak. "Rather, the lenses show you all probable futures from your point in time, where a particular question or event is concerned."

"Incredible! How do I use them?" I tapped the side impatiently and shook it, searching for some sort of lever or latch.

"That depends. What would you like to know?"

I paused and mulled his question over, debating possible questions. I figured it would be better to first test the lenses with a low-stakes inquiry.

"That harlot Naji has been harassing me to marry him. What would the future hold if I did?" I slipped the lenses over my face. The world fractured through them.

"Shut your eyes. Imagine his face. Imagine the ring on his hand. Imagine the contract signed. Then open your eyes," said Malak.

I did as Malak bid, imagining it all in as vivid detail as I could. I'm embarrassed to admit that the idea made my heart flutter. He would have looked nice beneath the light of a temple's oculus with a glint of gold on his finger.

Then I opened my eyes and saw through the lenses—

Naji and I in a lonely house by a great river, with three children until one falls in —

Naji and I, but we never had children or a house by a great river. We live in the gold district of Summer's Edge, in a grand house with everything money can buy. And I grow bored, and Naji grows bored and spends more and more time staring out the bedroom window, until one day he is gone—

Naji and I, but we never had a house, because I lost our money on a series of gambles, and the baby is hungry, and there's never enough of anything—

Naji and I, and we're never in one place long, I'm taking him to see the wonders of the world, but there are bandits on the road, one with a knife, a knife that he presses against Naji's throat and—

Naji and I, but he becomes entangled with another woman, and in a jealous rage I—

Naji and I, and we—

I ripped the lenses off with a gasp.

"What ... what did I ..." My hands were trembling so fiercely that I nearly dropped the lenses. It was as though I'd just lived seven different lives, decades of joys and tragedies packed into an instant.

"You saw the probable futures that would await you if you were to wed Naji," said Malak. It took me a moment to realize he'd even spoken, as I was still glancing around the chamber and trying to remind myself that I was in the Crystal Pyramid, not a house in the gold district or an inn in some foreign land.

"I don't understand," I said. "How can I know which one would be the true one?"

"This is a science even Empress Eru and her council struggled with," Malak said softly. He padded to the wall in which the Empress was entombed. He stared up at it with longing, as though he were speaking not only to me but to her, his voice drifting across death's veil. "She would use the lenses to see not just one divergence in time, as you did now, but dozens. Even hundreds. Through these exhaustive gazes into the futures, Empress Eru charted the events and decisions necessary for the best possible threads of time."

I raised an eyebrow. "Not well enough, clearly. Her empire is dead."

"Dead?" Malak tilted his head, and his metallic face seemed to shift into a grin. "Or sleeping?"

" 'Sleeping' would be a rather optimistic thing to call it."

Malak laughed and nodded to the right-most wall. "Look out into the sands again. What do you see?"

I looked out again at the desiccated peaks that peppered the dunes. I shrugged. "Pyramids buried in the sand."

"And in them, the Empire's millions, dreaming in their own glass cases." Malak looked away and again spoke up to Empress Eru. "She holds them in sleep with an enchantment that requires every fiber of her. When she takes her final breath, they shall wake."

"Final breath? She's *dead*!" I snapped at him. Malak said nothing, only continued to gaze into the crystalline wall. I turned my head to look as well, peering closer than I had before to prove to myself that Malak was talking nonsense.

Yet, encased in the crystal, I thought I saw the faintest rise and fall of her chest.

Malak spoke again. "She looked far into the futures, perhaps too far for her own good. She saw a great evil waiting a thousand years into every future. Something that could consume the world, Bazi."

"What could possibly be big enough to consume the world?"

"It is difficult to describe in terms you will understand." Malak paused and thought for a moment. "Imagine a grand house composed of countless rooms and chambers. They are built all around and on top of each other, with the base rooms supporting all the ones above. Now, imagine what would happen if a bitter carpenter were to take a hammer and begin making cracks in all the walls and beams of the base rooms, striking until they tore through. What would happen to the house?"

"Why, it would collapse, of course," I said.

"Precisely. Our world is one room among many. As we speak, a bitter carpenter in your continent is forging her hammer."

The words sank into my mind like stones. I couldn't think, couldn't speak. I merely stood dumbfounded until Malak spoke again.

"Empress Eru saw only a few hundred futures where the Empire survived this, but not one wherein she or her direct kin ruled. There were only a few hundred possible replacements suitable to lead her people out from the darkness."

"But why freeze everything? Why not just hand the crown off to them?" I asked. I watched the Empress breathe. The more I looked, the more of her I could see. Her eyes darted beneath their lids.

"They were not yet born," said Malak. "If she allowed the Empire to continue naturally until the candidates for the crown were of age, then she would someday die and events would spiral out of her control. There might be civil wars, deranged successors to the crown, or successors who would be either unwilling or unable to craft the time threads necessary. She could not exert sufficient control for those lands beyond the Empire's reach to narrow things down to a single perfect thread, but she could grant a fighting chance to the few hundred that would ensure the Empire's survival."

My breath caught in my chest as the truth loomed. "Those statues …"

"Any one of them could be where you stand now. Akeem, if he had not caught his illness as a child. Naji, if he had followed through on his fancy of stealing away with the maps the last night you spent together. Your mother, if she had never had you, and had instead apprenticed with a cartographer in her youth."

"Stop," I rasped. I turned away from Empress Eru and began pacing back and forth in the chamber, the lenses still dangling in my hand. The possibilities upon possibilities whirled in my head and drowned me. Had my years of efforts been meaningless, nothing more than bouts of cosmic luck? Had I ever had any power in my life at all?

"As I said, the Empire reawakens when Empress Eru draws her final breath. That final breath is drawn when you break the wall." Malak padded over to me. "You may attempt to do so with your hammer, or anything else in the chamber."

"I'm not attempting it at all! This is madness!" I stumbled away from him.

"Have you not spent all your life longing for wealth? Have you not craved power?" Malak continued to advance. "Every decision you have ever made has led you here. I know. I am the messenger, and my Empress has shown me all paths, yours included."

"You may have known I'd come, but you can't know my mind now. You can't know what I'll do."

Malak laughed, then nodded to the lenses in my hand. "Oh, Bazi. Of your path, we were the most certain. In every future from this point in time, you choose to take the crown. If you don't believe me, see for yourself."

I hesitated, the lenses poised in my hand.

"All you need to do is slip them on, imagine the crown upon your head, open your eyes, and see the futures."

I slipped them on. I imagined the crown upon my head. I opened my eyes. I saw the futures.

Every single one.

Every single blood-soaked battleground beneath my feet, every star stolen from a crimson sky, every daughter forged into demigod, every sword in my hand, every hollow laugh and savage cry, every added century welded to my life with sorcery, every death and rebirth and world upturned as I watched an empire rise from the ashes beneath my outstretched hand, wonders and terrors in my palm as I became something else.

And I screamed more than I ever had in my life.

I did not break the Empress' tomb or take the crown. I stashed the lenses into my satchel and fled. I didn't stop until I was out of the pyramid and riding away with Fig. Malak did not attempt to stop me, but I could hear his laugh following me all the journey home to Summer's Edge. I have not returned since.

But what I took in my bag was still enough to be life-changing. My old friend Akeem used his share of the riches to found the greatest trade company on the continent, managing it from the highest tower of the gold district. As for myself, well, look around. We sit together now on the balcony of the High Palace, with all the city-state sprawled out far below our feet. Terrified as I was of the lenses after my journey, I warmed up to them over the years and used them to craft the life I enjoy now.

No one in Summer's Edge is my equal. Not in wealth, not in power, not in love, not even in fame or esteem.

Sef, my husband, is gloriously handsome, charming, and fine, perfectly fine. They tell me my eldest daughter looks exactly like me, but she's got his fat nose. And the youngest does the same little snort when she laughs as he does. Horribly grating. I suppose I shouldn't speak ill of my family, though. I've been told they're perfect.

It's *all* very perfect, isn't it? I've reached the highest of heights in this city-state. I could smash the lenses right now and miss nothing. And you know, I thought about doing so, just a month ago. But first, I wanted one last look. For curiosity's sake.

I imagined the crown upon my head again.

And would you believe it, I wasn't anywhere near as terrified by what I saw as when I first did, fifteen years before. In fact, I was exhilarated. For here, in the palace of Summer's Edge with my family, I realize now that I am still only halfway up the sky. The material needs were fleeting after all.

And that's why I've brought you here. I'm told you're the best merchant to seek for supplying a long journey. Several hundred leagues across the sand wastes and all the Carmelian Seas to sail lie ahead, so I want the highest quality from your stock. Fig's not what she once was, so I'll be needing some new horses, ships, a sand-faring carriage ...

See Mia Ram's story "The Crystal Pyramid" online at Metaphorosis.
f you liked it, leave a comment. Authors love that!
Remember to subscribe to our e-mail updates so you'll know when new stories are posted.

About the story

I enjoy ekphrastic writing exercises (meaning writing that is based on an image or work of art) and this story is the result of one such exercise. I came across a painting of a shining, white pyramid while scrolling through a list of artworks and challenged myself to write a flash fiction about it as an exercise. That flash fiction grew into a full short story as I worked on it and began mentally adding layers to the story. What began as a page-long snippet about a traveler stranded in the desert is now the tale of a thief getting more than what she bargained for in her quest to raid an empress' tomb.

A question for the author

Q: What hero (of any gender) would you name your child after, if we lived in a society with names like that?

A: Moon Knight. It's a name that commands attention, both from peers and from ancient Egyptian gods. Moon Knight is a great namesake because he's a hero whose identity is in perpetual flux. He becomes whatever he needs to be in the moment, and that's the kind of philosophy I'd like to impart to the next generation. Fancy gadgets and super strength are all well and good, but true power is the power to adapt and change.

About the author

Mia Ram is a fantasy and science-fiction writer from Huntersville, North Carolina.

Frozen in Glass

Hope Davies

The first time Pinyit's father showed him the orbs in the shed, he'd been so frightened that he kicked and screamed the whole way down the garden path, right up until his father crouched down in front of him and gripped his shoulders tight, fingers digging into fresh bruises so hard that he winced.

"Listen, Pin," he said, voice kind but leaving no room for questions. *"When you're big, you'll be glad we did this. It's important to record the past so that we don't twist things around in our heads when we're older. You don't want that, do you?"*

"But what if it hurts?"

"It doesn't, I promise."

Inside the shed, there were rows upon rows of cracked wooden shelves loaded down with glass orbs. Some of the orbs were clear. Others were injected with colour, pinks swirling through blues, reds exploding in jagged lines, greens diffusing in soft, pleasant circles. When Pinyit reached out to touch one, his father smacked his hand away.

"Those are me and your Ma's memories. If you touch them, you might see something we don't want you to see, and that would be rude, wouldn't it?"

He bit his lip and nodded, chastened, but unable to take his eyes off the colourful orbs. He'd seen them both use the orbs before, their eyes closed as the colours seeped out of the orb, lighting up the air around them as they remembered things stored long ago.

His father picked him up and sat him down on a countertop, squished between the wall and a whole crate filled with clear orbs, a spider's web drooping perilously close to his head.

Pinyit craned his neck to watch as his father carefully selected a clear orb from the crate and pressed it into Pinyit's hands.

"Now remember what we said? Think really hard about something you want to remember forever, and it'll go into the orb!"

Pinyit looked at it doubtfully, *"And... it'll still be in my head too, won't it?"*

His father chuckled and ruffled his hair, *"Yes, it'll still be in your head too. And... one other thing."*

Pinyit met his father's eyes; amber-specked hazel turned to a cool shadow by the day's fading light.

"Make it something nice, Pin."

He did as his father asked, watching as green and yellow poured in thin streams from the places where skin touched glass. Sealed off and secure.

The truth, suspended in a moment of singular perfection.

Many years and many more orbs later, Pinyit stood in front of a different house entirely.

Manya's house was in the nicer part of the city. It was two stories where most dwellings were only one, wood panelling veined with glass that shifted with the heat of the day; wide and gaping, almost completely transparent during the cool mornings and evenings, then thicker and greener in the hot afternoons, making it harder for the sun to enter. Like most houses, it was propped up on short, chunky stilts that allowed air to circulate below, but instead of the bare, awkward hunks of wood or stone, these were lovingly polished and intricately carved.

It was a masterwork of craftsmanship, and Pinyit, with his painful, dust-caked feet and travel stained clothing, could not have looked more out of place if he tried.

One week on from The Incident, and Pinyit's ears still rang with Iq Shunyum's final words to him before his departure from the temple. *"You can come back when you can control your temper!"*

The Iq had used that biting tone, the same one he used when someone made a foolish mistake in a calculation or reshelved a book incorrectly. Close enough to what little Pinyit remembered of his mother's voice that he couldn't hear it and not flinch.

Pinyit never made foolish mistakes. He never reshelved books incorrectly. In fact, he had nearly three years' worth of stress headaches to show for the standard he had held himself to around Iq Shunyum. And then, in a single frayed moment, he'd made all that work count for nothing.

Carefully, he set his belongings down and knelt amongst the dry weeds at the house's base, where, inscribed into the wooden stilts, he found likenesses of the three moon goddesses: Killilla, Wuuiq, and Timah.

He got halfway through the prayers of protection before he remembered that, due to his failure to remain an Iq, it was inappropriate for him to be doing this.

His cheeks felt hot, and he hurried to his feet, brushing dirt from his trousers — yet another symbol of his fall in status. He knotted his fists in the fabric, painfully different to the calf-length robes he'd grown accustomed to in the temple, then forced himself to let go. He had to be calm. There could be no more 'incidents' if he wanted the temple to take him back. He had to be, in a word, perfect.

And he definitely wanted them to take him back.

The door opened and someone came down the steps.

It was Manya, long brown curls spilled across broad shoulders, black eyes alight at the mere sight of Pinyit.

"Did you get tired of being a priest already?" Manya asked, his voice light.

"More like they got tired of me." Pinyit breathed out hard, throat aching as he averted his gaze. He didn't want to be doing this. Begging his friend's parents for help again like he was still a child. He was supposed to have moved forward with his life. "Can I...?"

Manya's eyes grew soft. "Of course you can stay here. Come on in, Da's making dinner, it'll be ready soon."

Once inside, Manya led Pinyit first to the room that had been his since he was seven years old.

It was more or less exactly as he remembered it; bed pushed up against the window, drawers full of glass writing tablets scrubbed clean of practice equations and ready for use, three locked crates stacked in the corner, dust catching and collecting in the rough, splintered wood. From there, he found his eyes wandering over the wooden board nailed over the hole Pinyit had punched in the wall as a teenager.

"Oh wow, do you remember that?" Pinyit jumped a little at the sound of Manya's voice. "You were so *mad*."

"Yeah…" Pinyit said, quickly turning away. He bit the inside of his cheek. "Are your parents definitely okay with me being here?"

Manya stared at him in genuine confusion, "What? They're both thrilled, Da's been making his banana rice every night for the past *week* waiting for you to get back, ever since your letter arrived. Why would you think they wouldn't want you here?"

Pinyit wasn't sure he could put it into words, so he just shrugged and said, "Never mind, it doesn't matter."

In the kitchen, Manya's father, Lyhu, was hunched almost double over a cast iron pot, hair pulled out of his face, brown eyes hidden behind steamed-up spectacles that he pushed up onto his head when he saw the two of them.

"Evening, boys," he said, swiping at his brow with the sleeve of his cotton aprabe robe, "Pinyit, did Manya show you where we've been keeping your things?"

"It's all just in his room, Da," Manya interrupted, pulling a stack of mismatched glass bowls out of a cupboard, "We were up there literally five minutes ago."

Pinyit knotted his fingers in his sleeves and mumbled, "I still can't believe you kept everything."

Manya exchanged a glance with his father and then said, "Of course we did. Did you think we were going to throw all your stuff away the second you were gone?"

That was exactly what Pinyit had thought they would do. His mother had.

He remembered the smell of smoke more than anything else. Acrid. There were still white flecks of ash clinging to Lyhu's hair when he returned with nothing but the news that when he'd attempted to retrieve Pinyit's belongings, his mother had been in the midst of burning it all.

Pinyit hadn't cared at the time, and Lyhu hadn't pushed. It had only been a week since he moved in, and the healer was still giving him daily doses of powdered tyiim root to dull the pain of his broken wrist. Even now he could barely remember his mother, her existence confined to snatches of temper and the bone-deep awareness of his own cursed nature.

"Of course we didn't do that," Lyhu said, resuming his work, "You'll always have a place here, even if all you're using that place for is storage."

Lyhu had said some iteration of that same thing more times than Pinyit could count, but that didn't make it any easier to believe.

Pinyit soon fell back into the rhythm of helping, first going to the pot where fruit peels were kept and adding a generous helping to boiling water, then adding cinnamon, anise, and crushed peppercorns like Lyhu had taught him. He strained the fragrant tea that resulted out into the little cups Manya had set out.

No one was allowed to help with the rice itself, of course. It was Lyhu's pride and joy — soft and sweet, never too dry, and packed with beef marinated overnight in an earthy blend of spices that Lyhu promised he would teach Pinyit and Manya 'when they were ready'.

That evening, generous helpings were served, steam rising into the cooling air. About halfway through, Manya's mother, Cibree, arrived back from supervising work in the fields, barely pausing to wash the dirt from her hands before she began questioning Pinyit.

"So, what was it like at the temple? I bet their cooking wasn't as good as my Lyhu's," she said, pausing to elbow her husband lightly in the ribs. He grabbed her arm and tugged her in lightly for the combined purposes of giving her a peck on the cheek and rubbing a smudge of dirt from her chin.

"Let the boy eat, Cib," he chided, "He's only just sat down."

"It's alright," Pinyit said, unable to stop himself from tensing a little at Cibree's presence. "Their cooking *wasn't* as good as Lyhu's."

"Suck up," Manya muttered, but Pinyit saw the grin he was hiding behind his own bowl.

Pinyit shrugged, feigning ease. "You'd be sucking up too if you'd been living on nothing but qan porridge for two years." Just the mention was enough to have everyone's nose wrinkling.

"Did you like it there?" Cibree asked.

Pinyit felt his own smile start to strain. "It was good. They had some incredible resources, and it was good to have the senior Iqs there pushing us to work our hardest."

"Not too hard, I hope!" She swallowed a mouthful of rice. "I remember though —

that thing you were doing with the moons and the harvests."

Pinyit nodded. "Yeah, they brought over some tablets from Timah's temple — historical crop data. I know a lot of people say it's superstitious nonsense, but I noticed a real link between historical qan famines and periods with more empty skies."

Pinyit could've talked for hours about teaching himself the statistical techniques he'd needed but nobody at the temple knew, the natural history books he'd found and devoured, the rush of challenging himself to stretch outside the field he'd studied in to marry the various disciplines together.

But then Cibree said, "So, how long until you go back?"

The mouthful of food Pinyit had just taken lost all taste. He swallowed, then rubbed the yellowing bruise hidden under his sleeve.

"I'm not sure," he lied, "I felt like I needed a bit of time away."

Owning up to what had happened seemed an impossible task. From the moment Pinyit had been able to express a wish to study the skies, Lyhu and Cibree had done everything in their power to make it a reality. Cibree had leaned on her extensive network of contacts to find out exactly what Pinyit would need to do to be admitted to study in the temple. Lyhu had spent hours helping him work through calculations, literature, and required religious knowledge. Even Manya got involved, gleefully chasing Pinyit around and threatening him with everything from toads shoved down the back of his tunic to hiding all his shoes until Pinyit could answer perfectly whatever Manya was quizzing him on.

For them to find out now that he'd thrown all that away because he couldn't control his *temper*? They'd be devastated. He gripped his spoon a little tighter.

"Oh no, how come?" Cibree asked, voice flooded with a concern that only added to Pinyit's guilt.

"I, err..." He set down his bowl and wiped his sweating palms on his trousers.

"You know that you can talk to us about anything, dear," she said, wearing a smile that Pinyit knew she thought of as comforting, but only served to twist his heart around on itself.

"Leave it, Cib," Lyhu chided.

"If something's wrong—"

"How was work? That Klieri woman still giving you trouble?"

They launched into a spirited discussion about Cibree's ongoing dispute with one of her employees, and Pinyit kept his head down, focusing on eating his food as quickly as he could and pretending he didn't see Manya watching him the whole time.

After helping to clean up, Pinyit claimed exhaustion and went to bed early. Still too wound up to sleep, he lay on his side, staring out through the vein of glass running through his bedroom wall. At his touch, it widened and thinned, the opalescent turquoise fading almost entirely as it revealed a sky dappled with stars and a single moon, Killila. Wuuiq and Timah were hiding today, but he already knew that.

He knew the name of each and every star he could see and had dedicated years to charting them and tracking their movements across the sky. He knew that, in three days, there would be an empty sky — cursed, as the stories said.

Pinyit had been born under such a sky.

His father had told him once that it was why Pinyit was the way he was. It was why he cried so loud when he was a baby, why he was ill so often with stomach aches, why he could never seem to do as he was asked. A cursed sky made for a cursed boy, and there was only one way to deal with a cursed boy. His mother tried her best, his father frequently said, but sometimes it all just got the better of her.

What his father meant by that existed only in broad strokes in Pinyit's memory.

Violence, he knew, had been a part of it. As had yelling. He knew these things the same way he knew the names of the stars — the knowledge itself within easy reach, the memory of hours spent acquiring that knowledge lost to time.

He remembered his father's justifications more clearly than anything his mother had actually done, and they seethed beneath his skin like lightning.

When he couldn't lie still anymore, he jumped to his feet, began to pace, fingers snarling in his hair. He needed to hit something. To hurt. To get rid of the charge pulsing through him, driving him back and forth, back and forth across the room.

He forced himself to breathe.

From the corner of his eye, he caught sight of the crates, stacked one atop the other in the corner of his room. The day his father brought them to Manya's house had been the last time he and Pinyit saw each other.

Pinyit had been thirteen years old and unable to get through half a sentence without arguing with someone, battering himself against the lines set by Cibree and Lyhu, desperate to know if there was a crack, terrified he might find one. He hadn't seen either of his parents since coming to live at Manya's house, and the sight of his father with a push-cart full of crates had sent his mind spinning, careening back into a past he'd been trying to forget.

"What do you want?" Pinyit had said, taking his father aside whilst Lyhu looked on from the house.

His father was a little greyer than Pinyit remembered, trousers a little more creased. He had a splotchy new scar creeping up his cheek from under his beard and a habit of rubbing at it when he was uncomfortable.

He didn't smile when Pinyit spoke to him, just wearily said, *"You've a picture of us in your head now. No doubt influenced by that lot."* He tilted his head towards Manya's house. *"I brought the orbs in case you wanted to remember how things really were."*

Piniyt hadn't had anything to say to that. Just a tightening of his fists. A clenching of his jaw. A knowledge that this was his father and there was nothing Pinyit could do against him.

Now, Pinyit hauled the topmost crate down from the pile, knees buckling slightly under the weight.

Pinyit didn't know how to fix his temper, his inability to get anything right, or the mere fact of his birth under a sky shunned by the goddesses.

His memory though... maybe if he fixed that, patched up the holes, then the other things would start to fall into place around it. If he had specifics, he could pinpoint what, exactly, drove him into the kinds of rages that led to holes in the walls and being kicked out of temples. If he understood why it was there, then perhaps he would be able to anticipate the anger before it got him into trouble.

He dropped to his knees in front of the crate and attempted to pry open the lid several times before he remembered that it was locked.

Trying hard not to lose patience with his teenaged self, he retraced the favoured hiding places of that period; between the folds of clothing in his dresser, slotted into the dented casing of the first telescope Cibree and Lyhu had ever bought for him, in a wooden box filled with a strange collection of withered scraps of bark that had apparently caught the interest of his younger self.

Eventually, he thought to reach behind the dresser, feeling along the wall until his fingertips glanced across something metallic wedged into a crack. He worked it free and held it in a clenched fist, sharp edges digging into the palm of his hand as he withdrew his arm.

A rusty key.

He shuffled back over to the crate, slotted it into the lock and turned it.

The lid swung open, revealing rows upon rows of dusty glass orbs, loosely stacked, not labelled like the neat rows of similar orbs Lyhu and Cibree kept in their study. They glowed in the darkness, casting stripes of red, green, blue, and yellow across Pinyit's skin and clothing.

Few people in Kyhufut were as invested in the collection of memory orbs as Pinyit's father had been. Most people were wary of the debilitating hangovers that came with overuse of the orbs.

He'd created several whilst living at Manya's house, but he'd created hundreds under the direction of his father. Every few weeks, he'd sat and poured out copies of his memories into little glass balls no larger than oranges that were promptly secreted away into storage for when he was older.

He was older now.

He rubbed his sweaty palms on his knees. This was the only thing he could think of that would help. All he could do now was hope.

He rolled up his sleeves and grabbed the first orb he saw.

Glowing pink tendrils swirled within the orb, rushing up to meet the spot where Pinyit's fingers pressed up against the surface of the glass. A tingling, shrinking sensation banded across the inside of Pinyit's head as the pink matter surged out of the orb, wreathing his hand in light. The sensation intensified, the glow grew brighter, and he felt like he was suffocating, but then—

"Listen to this," Pinyit's mother told his Auntie Kihlush as they worked side by side, all three of them up to their elbows in

soapy water, "What do you want to be when you grow up, Pin?"

Pinyit knew this game, and it was an easy one, "I want to be an astro-astronimcaler!"

"An astronomer, just like his Da!" His mother grinned, and Pinyit glowed.

Oh.

Pinyit blinked the memory away and set the orb back down. He didn't know what he'd been expecting, but it wasn't *that*. He remembered now, his father's passing interest in astronomy, mapped out on glass tiles left scattered across the kitchen table.

She'd seemed so *proud* of him, she'd even been boasting about him to his aunt. That sense of joy and accomplishment lingered in his chest even now. Warm and bright. He didn't normally feel that way when he thought about his mother. It didn't make any sense. Didn't mesh with the image he had of her as rageful. Frightening. Willing to bruise and break.

Maybe another orb would provide some clarity?

The next orb he found had yellow pooled at its core like an egg. When he touched it, the memory seeped forwards, slowly enveloping his wrist.

"–and then Manya said that his Da said I could go to their house to play anytime I wanted!"

Pinyit trotted at his mother's side, struggling under a basket full of qan, sandals slapping loosely at his heels. She made a humming noise, not seeming to have fully understood what Pinyit was trying to ask.

"So can I?" he prompted.

"Can you what?"

"Go play at Manya's house?"

"Manya's parents are the ones who live in that big house at the edge of town, aren't they?" his mother asked, and Pinyit nodded vigorously.

"Yeah! It's huge!"

His mother smiled and ruffled his hair, "Of course you can go, sweetheart, I think you should definitely *keep* playing with Manya."

The orb hit the floor with a thud and rolled, yellow light arcing from Pinyit's hand, flooding back into the glass. He stared at it, panting for breath. That memory had been no different to the last one; it'd been so... normal.

He knew, in his gut, that his mother had not been as kind as the orbs were telling him. He'd had seven years with her and a whole twelve away to mull over and realise exactly why he was right to be frightened of her, but he couldn't ignore what the orbs were telling him, could he? His not understanding them didn't make the memories any less real.

He balled his shaking hands up into fists and stared hard into the box of orbs.

He moved past the orb filled with soft blue spirals, ignored the one with green waves rippling its interior. Dozens more he looked at and discarded, deciding they looked too soft, too unlikely to hold the harsh truths he craved. His eyes landed on one with vicious purple cracks running through its core. It looked… mean. Pinyit didn't know if there was any real correlation between the appearance of the orbs and the quality of the memories they held. He could only hope there was.

He picked it up. Braced himself. Let the past wash over him.

"Do you know what that one's called?" *his mother asked, pointing to the smallest moon in the cool evening sky.*

Pinyit shook his head. He'd never seen all three moons at once like this. His mother said it was rare, only happening once every three years.

"Her name is Killila," His mother said, "She's the youngest and she holds onto all of her sisters' joy whilst they work, just like you do for me and your Da." She beamed at him and pressed a kiss to his temple, her long black hair tickling his nose. "That's what Pinyit means. You're our joy."

The purple seeped back into the orb like fracture lines. If he didn't know better, he would have said it was broken. He didn't understand how all the orbs could be like... *this*. He knew that bad things had happened. He *knew* it. So why didn't the orbs show that? Pinyit stared at it, eyes damp, before he realised someone was knocking at the door.

"Come in!" he called out, hastily wiping his eyes on his sleeves. When he looked up, Manya was peering at him with a worried crease in his brow.

"I heard a bang..." The crease deepened as he took in the sight of Pinyit and the orbs, several of which were now on the floor, "What happened? Are these..." he crouched down, about to touch the orb full of red spines, but Pinyit quickly jumped to his feet.

"No! Don't!" he said, "I— it's private."

Manya pulled back, "Of course, sorry."

Pinyit crouched down, sleeve wrapped around his hand as he gathered up the spilled orbs, failing to get his ragged breath under control. He could feel Manya's gaze fixed on his back as he worked.

Pinyit put the lid back on the crate, plunging them into darkness. He sat with his back against his bed, hands screwed up by his sides. How was he supposed to hate his mother when, clearly, she'd loved him so much? And if she'd really been that kind, what excuse did he have for his failures?

Manya trod across the room, towering over him. Pinyit shied away, but then Manya sat down and pressed his warm shoulder into Pinyit's.

More silence.

"Go on then," Pinyit said when he couldn't bear it anymore, "Ask the question you've been dying to ask."

"What question?"

Pinyit rolled his eyes. "Don't act like you're stupid."

Manya straightened. "I'm serious. Enlighten me, what's this question that I've apparently been 'dying to ask'?"

Pinyit kept his eyes fixed on the moon dappled wall opposite. "Why did they kick me out?"

"What? I thought you were just joking when you said that."

Pinyit smiled ruefully and shook his head, "Nope."

Pinyit glanced towards Manya and saw him resting his chin on forearms crossed across his knees. It was such a quintessentially Manya-like gesture that Pinyit was momentarily taken aback. He really had been gone for a long time.

If he were at the temple right now, Iq Shunyum would likely be scolding him for laziness, *"If you've got time to rest, you've got time to clean."*

He'd pushed Pinyit to be the most capable version of himself, to learn things he never would have learned otherwise. Knowledge for its own sake, whatever the cost. And Pinyit had ruined it all over nothing.

"It was my own fault," he said, and Manya looked up, "I kept getting angry, and, well, you know how I am."

Both their eyes fell upon the boarded over hole.

"And then when it happened... I was talking to one of the senior researchers about my work, you know, with the cursed skies? And he said that it meant that maybe some people really *are* cursed. And then..." He rubbed the bruise on his arm. "Well, I smashed their telescope."

He didn't even remember doing it. Just white, searing anger. Then the lenses were cracked, the bronze was dented, and Iq Shunyum was staring at him, disappointment oozing like wax from a candle.

"That's it? You broke a telescope?"

"No, you don't understand," Pinyit said, shaking his head, "I broke *the* telescope. The Great One."

"Oh shit," Manya muttered.

"Exactly. They said — they said that if I could prove that I could control my temper, then I could come back."

"I thought that was getting better?" Manya said, "When we were kids you used to, err... get a bit wound up, but in that year before you left? I don't think I even heard you raise your voice. And I know you've not been back here long, but you remind me more of that Pinyit than the one who went round smashing stuff when he got mad."

Pinyit winced and couldn't help but let his gaze fall upon the hole in the wall again.

They'd both been fourteen when that happened. An argument with Cibree about something that in hindsight they both admitted was stupid. It would've been fine, but then she'd raised her voice.

Logically, he'd known that this was normal. People fought. *Pinyit* and *Cibree* fought. But something about the pitch or tenor of her voice that day had felt not like an argument with the woman who'd taken him in at his most desperate, but instead like standing on the beach, a wave as tall as he was about to wash over his head.

And then the wave had crashed.

He hadn't been trapped, but he felt like he was. Wasn't helpless either, or a child, or in danger, but that didn't matter. Heart pounding, face hot, something bitter in the back of his mouth. He might've shouted, but he didn't remember, too caught up in that visceral surge of rage tinged terror.

He'd stormed upstairs to his room and slammed the door so hard it shuddered in its frame. Yelled in frustration. It wasn't enough. Too much, too loud—

Stinging pain.

Wood buckling.

His fist had gone through the wall.

It was probably the worst thing he'd done whilst living with Manya's family. Afterwards, Lyhu had made him repair the damage himself, and then Cibree and Lyhu sat Pinyit down to have a long talk about things Pinyit could do when he was angry that didn't involve property damage.

It had helped. There were meditations he could do that worked, breathing with the goddesses in the same way the sea did. Focusing on his studies helped too. Anything that let him escape whatever situation he was in that felt like it was about to overwhelm him.

"It *was* getting better," Pinyit said, "I don't know what happened at the temple to change that, and that's a problem. What I was doing wasn't enough. I need to find something more."

Manya's eyes roamed once more back to the crate. "Is that what you were trying to do with the memory orbs? Figure out 'something more'?"

Pinyit nodded, then looked away, "They don't... They're not showing me what they're meant to."

"What do you mean?" Manya asked tentatively.

"They're all..." He couldn't look at Manya, kept his gaze fixed instead on his hands. There was still an ink stain, black crawling through the fine crevices normally invisible in his smooth brown skin, "They're all *good*. They show her being *good*."

"You're not..." Pinyit looked up to see Manya watching him with wide eyes, "You know your Ma was horrible, right?"

Pinyit nodded quickly, "I know, but in the orbs—"

Manya groaned in frustration, "Seriously? I don't know how much you remember from that night, but she *broke your wrist*. Before that, every time I saw you when we were kids you had some new story about 'falling down the stairs' or 'walking into a wall'."

"We were kids," Pinyit said, hoarse, "Kids are clumsy; maybe I did do all those things."

"Why can't you just accept that things are better here? You knew it when we were seven, why don't you know it now?"

"I do—"

"Then stop chasing after her! She didn't love you, Pin!" Shouting. Words that hit too close to bone. Pinyit's heart was pounding, his blood curdled hot in his face, the wave was rising, rising, rising—

"You don't get it," Pinyit said, controlled, perfectly controlled.

What did Manya know about love, anyway? He'd only ever tasted the uncomplicated kind, like an apple peeled and sliced and presented on a plate drizzled with honey. He'd never picked sharp spikes of peel from his gums, never gouged out soggy chunks of bruised flesh with his thumb. He didn't know that it was still the same apple, the same sweetness underneath.

"No! I don't get it! Those orbs," Manya gestured sharply at the crates and Pinyit tensed, "aren't proof of anything other than the fact that your Da decided to put something that can make *adults* sick in the hands of a three year old!"

He screwed his fists up. Manya's words echoing, *she didn't love you, she didn't love you, she didn't*—

It wasn't true.

Or it was.

Pinyit didn't even know himself, so who did Manya think he was, trying to decide for him? He tried to imagine the sea, breathing with the goddesses, but the images in his mind just crashed and frothed like waves cresting in a storm.

"Get... out." He hissed.

"Just think, for Timah's sake!"

"I said, get out!" Pinyit was on his feet; he couldn't stay sitting anymore, not when his blood burned and his heart thudded, so loud it seemed moments away from splintering his ribs with the force of it.

Manya, not shouting now, pursed his lips and nodded, getting to his feet so he was eye level with Pinyit, "Fine. Don't listen to me. Don't expect any sympathy when you mess yourself up."

Pinyit curled his fists so tight his nails, bitten short, sank into his palms. Manya walked away.

As Killilla and the stars travelled across the sky, Pinyit went back to the orbs. Maybe there was something he'd missed? There was a sliver of pain starting in the corner of his temple, but he ignored it and picked up the next orb.

A bright blue sky, his mother's hand—

The sliver widened to a splinter.

Constellations, his mother explaining that the Dog crawled from West to East as the seasons changed—

From a splinter, it grew into a shard.

Hours spent together, poring over glass writing tablets.

His head was pounding, and the entire right side of his face was on fire. Memories blurred into each other. Had that last one really been from an orb? Had it really been his mother? He remembered an almost identical scene from when Lyhu was helping him study for his entry into the temple. Without thinking, he pressed the cool surface of the glass to his cheek—

Soft, savoury qan cakes, crispy around the edges and buttered. He'd thrown up, and she always made qan cakes after he threw up. Food that wouldn't hurt his stomach, gentle like the hands she used to pull the blankets to his chin when she tucked him into bed.

"A good meal and some sleep and you'll feel better," she said.

He dropped the orb as another lance of pain pierced his temple. The room tilted, the floor falling out from beneath him until he fell prone, the walls spinning.

His heart beat painfully, and he was shaking all over.

The orb rolled away, the memories within condensing to thick grey smoke. His head had never hurt this badly in his life. He didn't know what to do anymore. He couldn't burden Manya's parents again, not like he'd burdened the temple, like he'd burdened his mother.

Another splinter of pain. He curled up small. Maybe they would forget about him if he was small.

She'd loved him, the orbs were *proof* that she'd loved him.

"Just think, for Timah's sake!"

Belatedly, Pinyit did.

The orbs came from his father.

"Make it something nice, Pin," he used to say. Every time.

Pinyit hadn't made many orbs since moving in with Manya's parents, but those few he had made were all stored together in the downstairs study.

And one...

He forced himself to stand, clinging to the wall when the floor seemed to tremble beneath his feet.

The veins of glass in the hallway were wide and open, glass stretched so thin it was almost transparent as, after a cool night, the house gasped for sunlight. Pinyit had to squint as he staggered down

the hallway, past the room shared by
Cibree and Lyhu, past the kitchen where
the big cooking pot had been left to soak,
past Manya's room, where Pinyit could
hear his friend moving restlessly in his
sleep.

He made it to the study, ignoring books
in favour of the shelves at the back of the
room which were loaded with dozens of
small wooden boxes, glass plates on the
front describing the contents in Cibree's
clear, straightforward hand.

Manya: third blessed sky one said, on
another was written *Cibree: nyltiut
ceremony.* He had to squint to read them
through the pain. Some of the boxes had a
small flower symbol indicating that it was
private. The labels for these tended to be
sadder, things like *Lyhu: mother's death*
or *Cibree: losing Hannyl.*

Pinyit wouldn't have been able to label
the memories from the crate so clearly if
he tried. After several minutes of
searching, he started to find boxes with
his own name on them. All of them had
the flower symbol, even the happier ones
such as *Pinyit: helping Lyhu in the kitchen
for the first time* and *Pinyit: acceptance into
the Temple of Wuuiq's Astronomical Order.*

He longed to open them up, to sit in the happiness he found in those years after his mother but before the temple. He couldn't.

It took a bit of shuffling things around and a lot of pausing when the pain in his head decided to remind him it was there, but he found what he was looking for at the very back of the shelves. A box just like the others, this time labelled *Pinyit: leaving parents*.

He remembered making this.

He'd been barely able to think through the Healer's medicine for his wrist, but Manya, strangely timid ever since Pinyit had turned up on his doorstep, had brought him a clear glass orb.

"My Da said that sometimes even really important things can be hard to remember if you're little when they happen or they're really scary. If you want to remember, though, put it in here and I'll keep it safe for you."

Pinyit didn't know what he'd put into the orb, but it seemed like the closest he would get. Something he'd created when it was still fresh, but when his father wasn't there prompting him.

He opened the box and pressed his fingers to the glass.

"*What do you mean you don't know? We talked about this yesterday.*"

Pinyit's mother smacked her hand down next to the tablet in front of them.

"*Lillina, leave him alone, these calculations are difficult for a child,*" his father said, head bent over his own work.

His mother scowled, "*Answer me, Pinyit. Why don't you know? Did you not study this after our lesson yesterday?*"

No, he hadn't. He'd gone outside to play with Manya instead. Stupid, stupid, stupid. He knew how difficult the stellar parallax calculations were. He should've practiced.

"*I asked you a question.*"

"*I… I didn't,*" he admitted.

Blotches on Ma's cheeks. Lips thin and narrow. "*Right. That's it. I've had enough of you. Get up.*"

She snatched his arm, ignoring his father's cry of, "*Lillina! Can't you see he's trying his best?*"

She pulled him to his feet, and marched him out of the kitchen, into the alleyway outside the house.

Two moons. Wuuiq and Timah. Both full and round, with a sliver of Killila just visible. The closest they were going to get to a blessed sky that year. Nothing really bad could happen with the goddesses watching so closely, right?

The wood panelling shuddered as Ma shoved him into the wall, both hands tight on his shoulders. She leaned in close, hissed, "What do you think you're playing at?"

He knew what came next.

"You're humiliating me. I don't expect much from you, Pinyit, but I do expect you to work."

Another slam. Pain gnawed through his back.

"Are you lazy?"

He shook his head.

"What, then? Is this just what you are? A nasty little boy? You've always been trouble. They warned me about you, you know that? A cursed brat makes a cursed house!"

Slam.

"Look at me when I'm speaking to you!"

She grabbed his hair, pulled his face back, leered. "Oh, now you're crying. Trying to make me feel like a bad mother. You should be grateful; I should have left you out on the beach for the goddesses to claim. That's what the other mothers do with your sort. I thought I could make you better than what you are."

Spit.

Cold dribbled down his face.

"Stop crying."

He couldn't.

"I said stop."

He wanted to.

"I said stop it!"

She wrenched him forward and he yelped, struggled to keep his balance before she shoved him back into the wall. His head whipped back, slammed into wood. No time to catch his breath before she ripped him forward again.

Pulled him so close that he could feel her breath on his ear, "I am sick of you trying to manipulate me." she hissed, and in a single motion, tossed him to the ground.

Hard earth caught his outstretched arm with a hard crack. Pain spliced through his wrist. He moaned, curling around the injury.

"Get out of my sight. I never want to see you again."

"Ma!"

"I said leave!"

Oh. Oh, goddesses. She *had* hated him, she—

"Timah's light!"

He hadn't heard the door opening, but there it was, and Manya was crouched in front of him, the orb rolling from slack fingers.

"Pin?" he said, voice high and urgent., "What happened?"

He screwed his eyes shut, why was it so *bright*?

"I'm getting Ma and Da," Manya said. "Just hold tight, you'll be okay."

"No," he muttered, reaching out to snatch at Manya's finely woven sleeve.

"What do you mean 'no'? You're a mess!"

He tried to shake his head, but it hurt too much. "You hate me."

Manya locked his jaw. "Don't be an idiot. I'm going."

The orb hangover lasted for four long days, most of which Pinyit spent unable to move without sending fresh waves of pain to scour the inside of his skull.

There was no curing overindulgence, but Lyhu spent the daylight hours with him, ready with a cold rag to press against the burning in his temple whenever he needed it.

Pinyit didn't talk much. He knew Lyhu was putting it down to his illness, but in truth, he was weighed down by that final memory. It had been one thing to know logically what his mother had done. To see glimpses of it in bouts of nervousness and anger, the details too painful to see more closely. Another entirely to relive it through the mind of his younger self.

Eventually, he asked Lyhu, "Do you think she loved me?"

Lyhu frowned a little, spectacles flickering with the reflection of the book of fine glass writing tablets he'd been reading from.

"That's not a question I can answer for you," he said eventually, setting his book down. "What do you think?"

Pinyit had had plenty of time to mull that question over on his own. He wasn't sure if he'd ever remember the full extent of what his life with his mother had been like, but he knew enough.

I never want to see you again.

He'd always known, deep down, what she was really like. The terror came with admitting it.

"I think... she loved the person she wanted me to be. When I was him, she loved me, and when I wasn't..."

In a way, that was what it had been like at the temple. Pinyit hadn't even realised how good he'd been at toeing that line, as adept at being the perfect student as he was at being the perfect son. Right up until that moment where he couldn't… when the constant battering of his defences had left them broken.

There was no easy fix for what had happened, for the anger. The only thing he could do was build himself back up again. Learn to truly tell the difference between those trying to help and those happy to tear him down.

Lyhu squeezed Pinyit's leg and, when it was apparent Pinyit was done talking, went back to his book.

Cibree tried one day to make qan cakes after work. She brought the still-warm plate up to him and said, "You've barely eaten, do you think you could try?"

He couldn't answer her. Tiny and round to make them easy for small hands and small mouths to manage. This was exactly how his mother used to make them.

"Oh dear," Cibree said, "What's wrong?"

He was crying. Pinyit wasn't sure if he'd ever cried in front of Cibree before.

Stop crying.

"I'm sorry," he said, hastily rubbing his eyes, "I don't want to be difficult. I'm sorry."

"Oh, sweetie." She sat down next to him, then seemed to hesitate before asking, "Can I hug you?"

He nodded, and she pulled him in, "You can be as difficult as you like, love, we're just glad to have you back."

It wasn't until Pinyit was firmly on the mend that Manya came to speak with him. "Can we talk?" he said.

Pinyit pulled himself into a sitting position and nodded, gritting his teeth against the churn of his stomach. Manya sat opposite, legs crossed. He opened his mouth to talk, but Pinyit quickly interjected, "I'm sorry I yelled at you. I shouldn't have lost my temper."

Manya worried his lower lip, then nodded. "You were upset. It's okay. And, well," He scratched the back of his head sheepishly. "I yelled first. I forgot how much you don't like that, so I'm sorry too."

"Thank you." Pinyit said, painfully aware of the part of him that would always be surprised at the sound of someone else's apology. "You were right, though."

Manya went still. "Yeah?"

Pinyit nodded, "About the orbs, it wasn't good for me to put so much faith in them. I don't know why my father wanted me to make them, but I think he might've been *trying* to get me to forget the bad stuff."

Pinyit didn't know whether his father genuinely thought it'd be better if Pinyit forgot what his childhood was really like, or if he was just trying to preserve his own ideal of what their family should look like. Happy, with a son who remembered a mother who taught him about the stars, not one who beat him.

"I think I can understand that," Manya said quietly. "I saw how miserable you looked going through those orbs and I just wanted you to stop."

"It didn't work, though," Pinyit said, "Thinking that she never did anything wrong just made me think I was broken. Or cursed, I guess."

His father had never tried to discourage that line of thinking either.

He'd been angry at his father for a long time, moreso now, knowing what had been waiting for him in the orbs. The feeling frightened him. There was a balance there that he was going to have to figure out. Between those who deserved that contempt like his mother and father, and those who were just unlucky enough to be caught by the tail end of it.

He pressed a hand to the vein of glass running close to his head and willed it to widen. Outside there was an empty sky, cursed, as the stories said, like Pinyit. For most of his life, Pinyit had been listening to the part of him that believed his mother when she said he was cursed, even if he didn't remember it. He'd thought, at the temple, that he could prove no such curse existed. As if qan harvests and the cycling of moons could quantify his own soul. Through the orbs, he'd tried to fix it. He knew better now. There was no external force that could prove or disprove the validity of his own experiences. He had to look to himself for that. To the people who loved him.

"Can I ask you a favour?"

"You already know you can stay—"

"Not that," Pinyit said, "The orbs." The crates had been sitting in the corner of the room for the past several days, untouched. "I want to put them in storage, make some room in here. Can you help me carry them?"

Manya smiled. "Of course."

See Hope Davies's story "Frozen in Glass" online at Metaphorosis.
If you liked it, leave a comment. Authors love that!
Remember to subscribe to our e-mail updates so you'll know when new stories are posted.

About the story

I first started thinking about writing a story about memory when I caught myself experiencing the phenomenon of false recollection. Someone was telling me about a picture that they'd previously shown me and, with a little prompting, I found that yes, I did remember what it looked like. Moments later, she pulled up a photograph on her phone of the picture she'd shown me, and I was fascinated to realise it was completely different to the picture I had been 'remembering'.

Of course, this is a pretty common thing that happens to everyone, whether we catch ourselves out or not, but nonetheless it got me thinking about what the purpose of memory is if it's so easily subverted by the suggestions of others. Many people crave a complete knowledge of the course of our own lives, it's why we curate photographs and journals, but our memory isn't set up with narrative totality in mind — it's there to keep us safely navigate a world too changeable for our genes to accurately predict and to help us connect with those around us.

This is when the thoughts I'd been having about memory collided with a worldbuilding concept I'd been playing around with for a while — that of glass that reveals the 'true nature' of a person. The thoughts merged, and eventually the glass became the memory orbs seen in "Frozen In Glass". From there, characters started to emerge as I began to think about what kind of conflicts and people could arise from this concept.

I started to think about what kinds of uses people have for memory, and more importantly, what kinds of forces play into the preservation and alteration of it. How might someone turn another person's own memories against them, not just internally, but externally as well? Why would they do that? When that happens, what does it take to disentangle the truth, and who do you trust — your current self, or the self who seems to be reaching out from the past to tell you a different story entirely?

A question for the author

Q: How do you generate story ideas, and how soon do you act on them?

A: My stories tend to come from things that have intrigued or bothered me — things I want to explore my own perspectives on, clarified by the lense of, usually, speculative fiction. When I get an idea, I tend to act on it fairly quickly, even if acting on it just means jotting down a sentence or a paragraph in a google doc. It tends to take much longer to work itself into an actual story though, and those early notes rarely bear much of a resemblance to the idea I end up committing to.

About the author

Hope is a speculative fiction writer from the UK.

hopedavies.blogspot.com, @Davies_Writes

Copyright

Title information

Metaphorosis August 2022

ISSN: 2573-136X (online)
ISBN: 978-1-64076-234-3 (e-book)
ISBN: 978-1-64076-235-0 (paperback)

Publisher

Metaphorosis
a magazine of | speculative fiction

Metaphorosis Magazine is an imprint of Metaphorosis Publishing
Neskowin, OR, USA

Discounts available

Substantial discounts are available for educational institutions, including writing workshops. Discounts are also available for quantity purchases. For details, contact Metaphorosis at metaphorosis.com/about

Metaphorosis Publishing

Metaphorosis offers beautifully written science fiction and fantasy. Our imprints include:

Metaphorosis Magazine
Plant Based Press
Verdage
Vestige

You can also find us:
@MetaphorosisMag, @Metaphorosis
www.facebook.com/metaphorosis

Help keep Metaphorosis running by supporting us at
Patreon.com/metaphorosis

See more about some of our books on the following pages.

Metaphorosis

a magazine of speculative fiction

Metaphorosis is an online speculative fiction magazine dedicated to quality writing. We publish an original story every week, along with author bios, interviews, and notes on story origins.

We also publish monthly print and e-book issues, as well as yearly Best of and Complete anthologies.

Come and see us online at magazine.Metaphorosis.com.

Plant Based Press

plant
based
press

Vegan-friendly science fiction and fantasy, including anthologies of the year's best SFF stories, from 2016-2020.

Chambers of the Heart

speculative stories
by
B. Morris Allen

A heart that's a building, a dog that's a program, a woman sinking irretrievably — stories about love, loss, and movement.

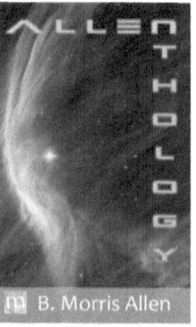

Susurrus

A darkly romantic story of magic, love, and suffering.

Allenthology: Volume I

Including three full collections of SFF stories.

Verdage

Science fiction and fantasy books for writers – full of great stories, often with an additional focus on the craft of speculative fiction writing.

Reading 5X5 x3

Changes

How do stories move from 'maybe' to published?

Here are 15 case studies of stories published in *Metaphorosis* magazine.

Reading 5X5 x2

Duets

How do authors' voices change when they collaborate?

A round-robin of five talented science fiction and fantasy authors collaborating with each other and writing solo.

Including stories by Evan Marcroft, David Gallay, J. Tynan Burke, L'Erin Ogle, and Douglas Anstruther.

Score

an SFF symphony

An anthology with an emotional score from the heights of joy to the depths of despair – but always with a little hope shining through.

Vestige

Novelettes, novellas, and novels by Metaphorosis authors.

The Nocturnals
Mariah Montoya

Night is Dangerous. Day is deadly.

Where day and night last thirty years, humans move constantly stay ahead of the night and cruel Nocturnals that call it home. But a boy is lost out there.